I0553418

THE KIDS AT GATOR LAKE

Micanopy Florida, July 1962

Leonard Dawson

CONTENTS

GATOR LAKE

My cousin Leigh's idea of fun was taking a leaky old rowboat out on the gator-infested swamp near her home in the middle of the night. She talked my sister and me and our other two cousins into sneaking out of their house sometime between very late at night and very early in the morning while their parents slept. Strung out in single file in the moonlight, the five of us trudged across Payne's Prairie toward the swamp they called a lake.

A long walk and a short boat ride later we were ankle deep in foul-smelling, black swampy water, bailing a sinking boat, and paddling frantically to escape two men chasing us. And that wasn't the only adventure Leigh talked us into during the summer of 1962, a hazy, crazy time that ended with us confronting a killer.

At nine years old, Leigh was the oldest of my three Ritchey cousins and the bravest of any of us. As tall as me even though she was a year younger, Leigh's brown hair was usually pulled back in a ponytail and tied off with a rubber band. A real tomboy, she would've cut her hair as short as mine if her mother had let her. She was dressed like a boy that night, wearing slacks and a shirt, which is how she always dressed except for church and special occasions.

When Leigh said words with an "O" in them, and certain other words like, "Y'all," she had a way of pulling her lips to the left, so she looked like one of the gangsters on television. Her

1

job that night was carrying the fishing poles. They were more like kids' toys than real fishing poles, but we didn't think the fish would know the difference. Walking fast, Leigh would get way out ahead of us then stop and yell, "Hurry up, y'all."

Leigh's younger brother, my eight-year-old cousin, Tripp, didn't have to carry anything, because his job was helping their little sister, Mattie, get through the barbed wire pasture fences. About an inch shorter than me, but really strong from years of doing farm chores, Tripp was as different from Leigh as Florida was from my home in Upstate New York.

Because Tripp had an overbite and his upper lip was naturally curled up a little, he seemed to be smiling all the time. That and his short blond hair, squarish face and freckles, made him look like the kid on the front cover of one of my parents' magazines; the one called, "The Saturday," something or other. Like the rest of us, he was wearing his dirty clothes from the day before. For Tripp that was a short-sleeved red and green plaid shirt, tan slacks, and a grass-stained pair of Keds.

I wore solid-color tee shirts most days because they were quick and easy, no buttons to waste time on. Mom didn't want me wearing shorts because of ticks, and I didn't want anyone checking me for them, so it was blue jeans. For speed I had a pair of broken-in Converse sneakers, and for my head, always a baseball cap.

My youngest cousin, six-year-old Mattie, had the long, wavy, golden hair of an angel and bright silver-gray eyes that sparkled like chandelier crystals when she smiled. I've heard people passing by her say things like, "Lordie, what a beautiful child," which gets Mattie giggling with delight.

So small she could hide behind her dad's easy chair standing up, I never saw Mattie wear anything but a dress, even when she helped Leigh and Tripp with chores on their ranch. She had a special pair of black shoes for church, but the rest of the time, even on the hottest summer days, she wore big, floppy, black rubber boots that had been Leigh's when they were new, then Tripp's until he outgrew them.

2

No matter what Tripp did to coax Mattie along that night, the two of them kept falling behind. I could tell Mattie was daydreaming from the way she pranced along looking down at her feet humming to herself. One time when they were half a pasture behind us I asked Leigh to wait for them. She refused, yelling at Mattie instead, threatening to leave her at home the next time they snuck off somewhere.

With a look of grim determination, Mattie ran to catch up with us, her tiny arms swinging stiff and straight at her sides like one of her dolls, her boots making slapping sounds against the skin of her calves. She and Tripp had almost caught up with us when Mattie slowed to a walk and went back to humming and prancing and falling behind.

Except for Leigh who was leading the way, we walked single-file, in order from oldest to youngest, the same order as tallest to shortest. At twelve years old, a year and a half older than me, my sister, Sarah, wasn't just the tallest and oldest, she was probably the smartest too, but there was no way I'd tell her that.

A whole head taller than me, she was the same height as Aunt Helen, our cousins' mother, who was short for a grownup. And Sis set her blond hair in curlers as big as the cardboard tubes in toilet paper rolls, which made it fluffy, and that made her look even taller. I once heard Mom tell her, that with her blond hair curled she looked like Marilyn Monroe. Of course, we all knew that wasn't even close to the truth.

A real honest-to-goodness bookworm, my sister spent most of her free time indoors between book covers and bedcovers. She was alright for a sister, except when she talked to me about grownup stuff like responsibility, and lately she'd been doing a lot of that. At Mom's last party she spent more time with the grownups than she did with us kids, and without even being told.

We brought two Chock-Full-of-Nuts coffee cans with us that night, Uncle Bud's favorite coffee. I carried the can filled with the nightcrawlers Tripp and I had dug up the night before.

Leigh gave the other can, which happened to be empty, to Sis to carry because my sister would never, ever, touch anything that had ever had any actual dirt in it. When Sis asked Leigh why we needed the empty can. Leigh wouldn't say. She just smiled.

* * * *

I soon saw the lake in the distance, shimmering in the moonlight like a gigantic black jewel, its sinister-looking dark expanse stretching so far into the distance I couldn't see the line between it and the night sky.

My cousins had always called it "The Lake," so that's what I'd expected to find. But I'd seen enough swamps on television to know that their lake was one of them, plain and simple, right down to the lumpy, puke-green scum covering it.

It looked like the kind of place where monsters lurk, waiting for some stupid kids to come along and be their dinner. So, yeah, I was scared to go out there in a boat. But I hid it because I'd just die of embarrassment if my cousins found out, especially Leigh.

THE DAY WE ARRIVED IN FLORIDA

We traveled from Central New York to Florida every summer to visit our relatives, usually staying with them for a month or more. My sister and I stayed with our cousins, the Ritcheys, most of the time. Their mom and our mom were sisters, although you couldn't tell by looking at them.

Sometimes I stayed with my dad's parents, the Dawsons, and sometimes my sister stayed with my mom's parents, the Thurmans. My dad, who was a professor at Cornell, didn't come with us that summer. He stayed home to work, which had to be easier without Sis and me bothering him.

That year our visit started out with Sis and me both staying at the Ritcheys', who lived in a long white ranch house with about a thousand mud wasp nests under the edge of their roof. And they had a circular driveway as long as a football field, something we didn't have up north because you couldn't possibly shovel all that after a snow storm. You'd have to wait for spring. Cattle pastures and barbed wire fences marked the other three sides of their yard.

The day we arrived, Uncle Bud and my cousins came outside to greet us. Uncle bud was over six feet tall and had a way of standing with his fists on his hips. That's how he was waiting for us that day, with his light-brown hair that looked like short, fine, curly wire, and his wide squarish face that was

5

always reddish and freckled from working out in the sun. Mostly he wore work shirts like my grandpa Dawson, but compared to Grandpa's, Uncle Bud's were worn-out looking. He looked like a giant standing next to my cousin Mattie.

The first thing he did was give my mother a hug. Then the two of them went through some silly grownup stuff, like him saying, "Oh, Lizbeth, you look pretty as a picture," which she didn't, and her saying, "You don't look a day older," which he did.

Instead of calling my mother by her real name, "Elisabeth", my aunt and uncle called her "Lizbeth." Mom told us that was left over from when she and Aunt Helen were kids.

When Uncle Bud looked at my sister he put his hand on his chest and pretended to be surprised. "My goodness, Sarah, but you sure have grown. I do believe you're taller than Helen now."

Sis didn't say anything. She just blushed, which I enjoyed immensely.

Then Uncle Bud held his hand out for me to shake. "Hello Lainard."

Because of their heavy southern accents, Uncle Bud and Aunt Helen said my name so that the "Leon" part, which should sound like "Len," ended up sounding like a nasally "Lain." My name didn't sound nearly as bad when one of my cousins said it.

Uncle Bud shook my hand, the only grownup besides Grandpa Dawson to ever do that. He even bent over a little to make it easier for me to reach his hand, which was the size of a baseball mitt and rough as sandpaper, not at all like my dad's.

Leigh said, "Hey, y'all."

Tripp smiled and mumbled something. Quiet as lump, Mattie watched her feet as she twisted left and right. Uncle Bud suggested we all go inside. Leigh led the way into the kitchen where Aunt Helen was cooking something. "Oh Lizbeth," Helen said, "forgive me for not being out there to greet you. I was afraid I'd burn the chicken, and I know y'all don't want chicken cinders for dinner."

Aunt Helen and my mom looked more like friends than sisters. My mom had long wavy blond hair and eyes the same color as mine, which she says are hazel. Aunt Helen, with her frizzy dark hair and dark skin looked like a kid at my school who came from somewhere overseas.

My mom was almost a foot taller than Aunt Helen. And Aunt Helen always wore flip-flops at home which made her seem even shorter. My mom never wore flip-flops. That day Aunt Helen had on a black dress with four big white buttons in the front and a white collar. Thick as a blanket, Mom's pink plaid suit looked much too hot for Florida.

After the two of them hugged, Mom told Aunt Helen she wasn't staying for dinner, that she was going to their mother's house, my grandmother Thurman's, for dinner. Try as they might, Aunt Helen and Uncle Bud couldn't talk my mother into staying.

The Ritcheys' kitchen and family room was one long connected room. The fish tank in the family room was the first thing I noticed. You couldn't miss it – it was as big as an overseas trunk. I checked out the fish because that was easier than talking to my cousins whom I hadn't seen for a year, and a year is a very long time when you're ten years old.

As it turned out there weren't any fish in the tank, just a baby alligator about as long as both of my hands stretched out thumb-to-thumb. Either it was doing a Deadman's float or it was actually dead. I bent down close to the glass, just an inch or two from the little reptile. It didn't move, not even when I tapped on the glass, but I swear its tiny black eyes were watching me. I wondered what it was thinking, wondered if it thought I looked like dinner, or if it was playing dead because it was afraid of being my dinner. I asked Leigh where they got it.

"Y'all remember the lake?"

I shook my head. I remembered my cousins talking about it, but didn't remember ever seeing it.

"Some men who came to hunt gators found a nest with eggs in it."

The idea that there really were alligators in their lake should have sunk in, but it didn't. I imagined a full grown alligator in their family room. "Won't it get awfully big?"

"Oh, we're not gonna keep it. Mattie's gonna take it in for 'Show and Tell' when school starts this fall. We'll let it go in the lake after that."

Aunt Helen told us kids, "Y'all go wash up for dinner."

She seldom smiled, and when she did she looked so uncomfortable you'd have thought it hurt. Leigh, who was standing closest to the hallway door started for the bathroom first, walking faster when she saw Mattie getting up. Mattie ran into the hall, quickly getting ahead of Leigh. Leigh ran after her.

Aunt Helen yelled, "No running in the house."

I could hear the girls giggling and running.

Aunt Helen yelled, "What'd I tell you about running in the house?" then shook her head as she turned her attention back to a pot on the stove, muttering to herself, "How many times do I have to tell them?"

From the hallway, I saw Leigh pushing her way into the bathroom ahead of Mattie, who told her, "No fair; I beat you," to which Leigh replied, "Doesn't matter."

When I got there Leigh was washing her hands. Mattie was standing with her fists balled up on her hips scowling at her sister.

Leigh swiped her hands once on the towel hanging on the door before leaving.

"Hey," Mattie yelled after her, "what about my stool?"

Tripp and I had been waiting in the hallway. He said Leigh's name so it sounded like a complaint as she walked past us. Leigh ignored him. Tripp was getting the stool down off the laundry shelf for Mattie when Sis showed up. He told her to go ahead. When she was done he waited for me to wash my hands before he put the stool on the floor in front of the sink for Mattie. Then he handed her the soap. Standing on the stool, stretching her arms out full length, she could just reach the faucet handles. I toweled off and left. We were all sitting at the table when Tripp finally joined us. Leigh grinned at him, called him a slowpoke.

Before bowing her head to say grace, Aunt Helen glanced

at Tripp, "We're always waiting dinner on you, Tripp."

MATTIE AND THE PIXIES

Stopped here

After dinner Aunt Helen told us kids to go outside and play. Before you could say, "Jack Robinson," Leigh was racing Tripp to the back door.

Even though Aunt Helen yelled, "Hey," the moment she turned her back Mattie ran for the door. I was too afraid of getting yelled at to run. My sister, Miss Goody-Two-Shoes, would never, ever do anything like that.

We all laid back in the grass to watch some vultures circling over something. I didn't wear a watch, so until my shadow was fifteen feet long, or the sun set, or someone called me in for dinner, I had no idea what time it was. And with no sense of time passing it felt as though the wonderful lazy days of summer would last forever.

After a while a dog came racing around the end of the house then ran circles around us barking up a storm. It looked like my friend's Irish Setter back home, except that it was black and tan instead of red. I told Tripp his dog was crazy.

"That's Dana. He's a stray my parents took in. He goes with Dad when Dad feeds the cattle."

"He herds the cattle like sheep?"

"Nah, he mostly just barks at them."

Dana came over to me slowly, with his head down and

his tail almost between his legs. I held my hand out. He sniffed it. I patted him once on the head. His tail wagged once then he trotted over to Mattie, wagging his tail so hard his whole backside wiggled. She patted the ground. Dana curled up in the grass next to her, his tail thumping the ground hard enough for me to hear. She rested her head on his stomach.

Except for a squirrel chittering about something it didn't like, it was quiet until Sis asked Mattie what she wanted to be when she grew up.

"I want to be a princess and live in a castle in the clouds. And I want to wear the prettiest dresses and have the sparkliest jewels. And I want to have a fairy godmother, because they won't let anything bad happen to you."

Leigh told her she was being silly.

"Am not."

"There's no such thing as a fairy godmother."

"Is too."

"And you'll never be a princess."

"Poop on you, dummy-head."

Sis asked Leigh if she'd ever heard of Grace Kelly.

"Who?"

"The movie actress who became a princess."

"Now you're being silly."

"No, it's true. She married the prince of Monaco, and that made her a real princess."

Mattie stuck her tongue out at Leigh and said, "Not so smart now, are you?"

"Smarter than you."

After that we looked for shapes in the clouds until the sun set and the fireflies came out. We chased them and Dana chased us, barking up a storm. After trying unsuccessfully to catch one for herself Mattie asked Sis to catch one for her.

Moments later I heard Sis say, "Ooh, Mattie, come here. I've got one."

The way Mattie ran over to her with her little arms and legs flailing and her face beaming with expectation, you'd have thought Sis was giving her a puppy. Sis opened her fist a crack to let Mattie peek in.

"Phooey" wasn't the reaction Sis was expecting. "What's wrong, Mattie?"

"It's not a Pixy."

Leigh told her that fireflies were just bugs.

Scrunching her face up into an angry frown, Mattie said, "Are not" then asked Sis to catch another one. Sis caught a passel of them, and for every one she showed Mattie, the poor kid got more disappointed until she cried about it. A flood of apologies from Sis didn't stop the crying.

Lucky for Sis, that's when Aunt Helen stuck her head out the back door and called us in for bed. As we filed past her she told us that in China fishermen used to fill jars with fireflies for lanterns. I thought that was pretty cool, but no one else seemed to.

Head down and pouty-lipped, Mattie came in last. Aunt Helen asked her what was wrong.

"I didn't get a pixie."

"Well, tomorrow's another day. Now hurry up. You're letting the mosquitoes in."

I had trouble getting to sleep that night because it was so warm my bedsheets stuck to my skin, so warm my pillow felt hot even after I flipped it over.

Having given up trying to sleep, I asked Tripp, "Your uncle's the sheriff, isn't he?"

I already knew the answer because there was a picture of him in his uniform on the wall by their dining room table. But it got Tripp talking, well sort of. The "yeah" I heard out of the darkness across the room sounded pretty sleepy.

I asked Tripp if his uncle wore a badge.

"When he's wearing his uniform."

"What about a gun?"

"Sometimes."

My next question was the one I'd wanted to ask all along. "Did your uncle ever shoot anybody?"

Tripp said he didn't know.

"You never asked him?"

"Nah."

"How come?"

"I don't know. I guess because he's my uncle. I don't think of him as a sheriff."

I had asked my grandpa Dawson lots of questions about being a boxer and a fireman. I would've asked him even more questions if he'd been a sheriff. I heard Tripp snoring then.

WE'RE GOING

Sneaking out to the lake was all Leigh's idea. She talked us into it one morning when the five of us were playing croquet in their back yard. It was one of those warm sunny days in the dead of summer when school was still a million years away.

Poor Mattie's croquet ball would either barely move or her mallet would glance off of it sideways. She had so much trouble getting it through the starter hoops that none of us complained when she picked it up and threw it. She couldn't throw it very far anyway.

After a while it got so hot we stopped playing to get a drink from the garden hose. Tripp hooked the hose up and handed it to Sis. I suppose he was being nice letting her go first, but she drank from the hose as soon as he turned the water on. She spit it out immediately, and my sister was not a spitter. She'd obviously never taken a drink from a garden hose before and didn't know the water would be warm and rubbery tasting from the sun shining on it.

While Tripp explained that to her, Leigh pulled me aside and asked, "Do you want to sneak out some night to go fishing at the lake?"

I was about to say, "No," because if we got caught I'd be grounded forever, and I always got caught when I did something I shouldn't, but then Leigh told me, "Your sister said she'd go."

Then I had to go. I didn't want my cousins to think Sis was braver than me.

Later, while Tripp was taking his turn getting a drink, I

heard Leigh ask Sis if she wanted to go and I knew she'd tricked me. Of course, Sarah would refuse to go. She would never, ever do anything that involved worms. The most outdoorsy things she ever did was go on Mom's family picnics, which weren't very outdoorsy. So I didn't have to worry about backing out and looking like a chicken, because Sis would refuse to go and Leigh would give up on the idea.

But when Leigh asked Sis to come with us, Sis said, "Yeah, sure," as though it was no big deal.

So I had to go after all. Of course Sis would regret it. I had no doubts about that. But I kept my mouth shut because it would be loads of fun when something happened that she didn't expect, like drinking from a garden hose without waiting for the water to run cold.

Leigh asked Tripp next. The way he shook his head you'd have thought she'd asked him to lick her boots.

She promised she'd be nice to him "for ever and ever."

Tripp shook his head again.

Pretending to get a drink from the hose she squirted him with it instead by holding her thumb over the nozzle. Tripp ran until she couldn't reach him with the water, but his back was soaked. She called him a pansy. He said he wasn't going.

Mattie, who was kneeling in the grass poking a beetle with a blade of grass, jumped up and down and clapped her hands and yelled, "Squirt me, Leigh, please."

Leigh ignored her. Mattie tugged on Leigh's pants, told her she wanted to go fishing with us. Leigh told her no, in what my mother would have called "no uncertain terms." Mattie scrunched up her face. A tear left a glistening streak where it ran down her cheek.

Leigh shook her head in exasperation. "Okay, but if Mom comes out and gives me hell for making you cry you're never going anywhere with us."

Mattie sniffled and wiped her face with the back of her hand. After wetting her shirtsleeve with the hose Leigh told Mattie to hold still then wiped her face.

Mattie cried, "Owie."

Leigh told her to be quiet then knelt down so her face was just inches from Mattie's. "You gotta promise me you won't tell Momma that we're going to the lake."

Mattie nodded her head.

Leigh tipped her head, looked at Mattie sideways and squinted. "Cross your heart and hope to spit?"

Mattie made a show of drawing a big "X" on her chest with her thumb then bent over to spit. Nothing came out but she did a good job of faking the sound.

In the meantime Tripp had snuck around behind Leigh toward the back door while we'd been distracted by Mattie. But with her taken care of, Leigh turned her attention back to Tripp. He wasn't close enough to the back door to make it without getting wet and he couldn't go in the front door and through the living room with wet clothes.

When Leigh saw him she said his name as though it was two syllables, her voice sliding up half an octave between saying "Chee" and "up."

He froze. She promised she wouldn't squirt him. I can't imagine why he trusted her, but Tripp took a step closer to her then stopped, testing her I suppose. He took a few more steps, stopping when he was close enough for them to talk quietly, because with the kitchen window open Aunt Helen might hear them. Leigh told him he had to come with us because Mattie was going.

Tripp got as far as saying, "If Mom and Dad find out..." before Leigh interrupted him. "How are they gonna find out?"

"I don't know, but they'll skin us alive if they do."

She rolled her eyes. "It's only a spanking. It won't kill you."

Tripp told Leigh that Mattie couldn't go anyway.

"Why not?"

"She can't swim."

"Cain too," Mattie said, knitting her brow and putting her tight-fisted little hands on her hips the way my mother did when she was mad at me.

16

"Can not," Tripp said.

Mattie began chanting, "Liar, liar, pants on fire."

"Hush up," Leigh said, putting her hand over Mattie's mouth. "Momma's gonna hear you."

Sis put her two cents in. "Leigh, I think Tripp's right. Mattie shouldn't go if she can't swim."

"See," Tripp said, as though Sis saying it made it so.

Most kids thought Sis was super smart. I knew better, but before I could tell that to my cousins Leigh started chanting, "Trippy is a pansy," and Mattie joined in.

It wasn't long before poor Tripp gave in and agreed to go, which meant I'd be going to the lake for sure. At least we hadn't decided on a day yet, so something could still come up that would keep us from going. I could always hope so.

While Leigh was warning Mattie again not to tell anyone about going to the lake, especially their parents, Tripp grabbed the hose from Leigh and squirted her, and from only two feet away. He had to know that would get him in beg trouble.

Leigh ran for the back door yelling, "Momma, Tripp squirted me with the hose."

Aunt Helen appeared on the back stoop an instant later. Tripp told her that Leigh had squirted him first.

Aunt Helen did the same thing Mattie had just done – knitting her brow and putting her tight-fisted hands on her hips. "Well then I reckon you can both come in."

That left Mattie and Sis and me outside trying to think of something to do. To keep Mattie happy we played hide-and-seek for a while. It wasn't my favorite game, but it was something Mattie could play, well sort of. She used the same hiding place every time, and like an ostrich some part of her was always showing, usually her butt.

We'd been playing that forever when Aunt Helen rescued Sis and me by sending Leigh and Tripp out with a plate of peanut butter and jelly sandwiches. You can't beat PBJs on soft white bread, especially when they've been cut into triangles.

After checking for red ant mounds, all of us, even Sis, sat

in the grass to eat. Humming something between bites, Mattie was soon distracted by a bee that landed on a dandelion next to her foot. She put her sandwich down in the grass and reached for the stem under the bee. Lucky for her, the bee flew away when she touched the stem.

Mattie made a pouty face. Then she picked up her sandwich and looked it over, brushing off a big black ant and a few blades of grass from yesterday's lawn mowing before taking a bite. It's easy to squeeze jelly out of a PBJ, even for Mattie's tiny fingers, and sure enough, a big blue glob of grape jelly fell out of her sandwich and landed on her bare knee.

Putting her sandwich down in the grass again she lifted her knee up to her mouth by pulling on it with both hands then licked the jelly off, and a little dirt with it.

Leigh said, "Yuck, Mattie, don't do that."

Just when Mattie stuck her tongue out at Leigh, Aunt Helen magically appeared on the back stoop to tell her. "That's not something we do, young lady."

Of course, it wasn't really magic. Aunt Helen had come out to get Sis and me. "Lainard, you and Sarah need to come in and get cleaned up. Lizbeth will be here soon to pick you up."

TROUBLE WITH TOMMY LEE

Aunt Helen told me to take a bath and put on clean clothes, which meant Mother had something planned that I wouldn't like. Sure enough, when mom showed up she had on her special occasion dress, the white one with big orange flowers. I once heard Mom tell Sis that the flower was called Bird of Paradise, or some such nonsense.

Mom had her long wavy blond hair curled up on her head in a swirl like a cinnamon bun. She never wore it that way in New York. It felt cooler, I guess. Anyway, that by itself wasn't the worrisome thing. It was not seeing any loose strands of hair hanging down, which meant she'd spent extra time putting it up, which meant I'd be miserable for sure.

And then there was her necklace, a handful of light green stones the size of peas on an old worn piece of stuff that looked like string. I once told her that it looked like string. She told me it was very old and that her dad, my grandfather Thurman, brought the necklace back from China, which is why Mom only wore it on special occasions, the kind I didn't like.

So there I was smelling of soap, wearing a stiff shirt, and pants with no grass stains, sitting in the car with Mom in the Ritcheys' driveway waiting for Sis. I asked her where we were going.

"To the Dawsons'."

I'd been to the Dawsons' plenty of times without ever once dressing up. "How come I have to wear church clothes to go there? I never did before."

"Because there'll be people there today that we haven't seen in years."

And there it was – a day with strangers. Who could blame me for complaining? "Aw Mom, why can't I stay here?"

"You're going, and that's that."

"But, Mom, you know I hate that stuff."

"What did I just say, Buster?"

That's what my mother called me when she was mad at me. But it didn't matter because Sis came out then and Mom started the car, so like it or not, I was going.

Grandma and Grandpa Dawson lived in a little house on the other side of Gainesville. Their whole living room wasn't much bigger than my bedroom back home. Because the three cars parked in their driveway filled it, Mom parked on the grass under the big live oak tree in Grandpa's front yard. As we pulled in I saw a kid about my age sitting in a rocking chair on their front porch. I asked Mom if I could stay outside with him.

"You can come back out after you've said hello to everyone."

Grandpa's house was packed with people I didn't know, and most of them were old. He and three other men who looked as old as him, were sitting in the living room. Grandpa was wearing a blue workingman's shirt and pants, which is what he always wore, except for special occasions when he wore what he liked to call his "funeral suit."

Grandpa was always bent over, something to do with his back. And he always had a suntan. My dad never had a tan. Compared to my dad, Grandpa was skinny. Maybe that's why Grandpa wore his belt above where his waist ought to be, which looked funny.

He and my dad had both lost most of their hair. Grandpa had a thin halo of gray hair. His head looked shiny without his straw hat, which he called a boater, and which he almost always wore, except at the dinner table. My dad still had a few strands of hair on top of his head. Grandpa didn't need glasses. I couldn't remember my Dad without his.

Dad smoked cherry flavored tobacco in fancy metal-stemmed pipes that he lit with a Zippo. I liked the smell of the tobacco. Grandpa smoked a blackened corncob pipe which he lit with big wooden matches. He lit the matches by scraping them with his thumbnail. His pipe was always in his mouth, even when he was talking.

Grandpa's front shirt pocket sagged from the can of Sir Walter Raleigh tobacco in it, the only kind he ever smoked. He and Grandma used the empty cans for target practice with their pistol. They let me go with them once. Of course, I never told Mom or Dad about that. Anyway, Grandpa would get lucky and hit Sir Walter once in a while. Grandma never missed.

When he was a lot younger Grandpa had been a boxer called "Sugar Boy Dawson," which I thought was extra super cool. Later he became a fireman, had even made it to assistant fire chief before he retired. My dad was a professor at Cornell. He knew lots of scientific stuff I didn't understand and or care about. But Grandpa knew important stuff, like how to catch a fish and clean it, and he could fix just about anything, even cars. But the best part of staying at his house was that I could talk to him about anything. Visiting Grandpa was like having a big brother for one month every summer.

Grandma was sitting at the dining room table with three old ladies and an old man. All of them as old as her, maybe older, and all of them with wrinkly faces. One of them had dirty fingernails. But not my Grandma, hers were always squeaky clean.

Not much taller than me but bigger around the middle, Grandma always had a smile for Sis and me. Like Mom she had her hair pinned up on her head that day, but one big white strand of it had gotten loose and was hanging over her ear. Grandma always wore a small locket on a thin gold chain. One time she opened it up to show me the tiny picture of her wedding day that she kept in it.

The old guy sitting with the women had a darker tan than Grandpa. Muscles rippled in his forearms even when he did something as easy as stirring his coffee, so I figured he had a pretty hard job, like farming.

Pointing at him with her thumb, Grandma said, "Buster, this here's Dude Dawson."

I didn't like Grandma calling me Buster, but it was better than being called Dude. I didn't like meeting grownups, but I'd catch hell from Mom if I wasn't polite, so I held my hand out for him to shake and said, "Nice to meet you, sir," being extra careful not to smirk because of his name.

Dude glared at me. I couldn't imagine what I'd done to make him angry, but I was always doing dumb things around grownups and getting in trouble for it. Then Grandma said, "Dude here is your great aunt."

My face turned as red as a ripe tomato. I knew it did because my cheeks were on fire. How was I supposed to know he was a woman? She had a man's name. And she looked like a skinny old man with a dark farmer's tan wearing work pants and a work shirt, and if that wasn't enough, she was chewing tobacco. Women didn't do that. Actually, I thought she was chewing gum until she spit a big dark-brown glob of tobacco juice into one of the coffee cans Grandpa kept around the house for pipe ashes.

Grandma introduced me to her other friends, but I didn't much care about second cousins twice-removed, or whatever they were. They were all looking at a book of old photographs and talking about the people in the pictures, about which ones had died and when. Then they'd talk about the kids and where they lived and how many kids their kids had. But I didn't want to look at pictures of people I didn't know, especially dead people I didn't know. So the next time Mom wasn't looking I told them I had to get something out of the car and snuck outside.

The kid on the porch told me his name was Tommy Lee.

When I told him my name he said I talked funny and asked me where I was from. Even though Tommy Lee was in sixth grade, one grade ahead of me in school, we did have one thing in common – we both liked Popular Science magazine.

We got talking about the one he'd brought one with him, an issue with predictions about the future. Sitting in Grandpa's rocking chairs we talked about nuclear cars and jet packs and television phones. According to Popular Science that stuff would be around by the time we were grownups, which seemed about as likely as me becoming president.

A PRETTY GIRL

After a while the Petersons, whom I hadn't seen since the summer before, showed up with their five kids. I wondered what it would be like living with four other kids, imagined fighting over toys, wondered if their parents had enough money to give them all nice presents at Christmas, and wondered who decided what they watched on television.

Mrs. Peterson had on the brightest red lipstick I think I'd ever seen, and her brown hair was pulled back and held in place with two of those things women stick in their hair that look like combs. She was a nice lady, almost as nice as Grandma Dawson.

But not Mr. Peterson. He scowled at me when I shook his hand, even before I had a chance to do something wrong. Staring down at me with eyes like the black marbles in a Chinese checkers set, he gave me the willies. He had one of those thin straight mustaches, something I could've drawn on with a black magic marker. Mom once told me that he was a fighter pilot in World War II, that he'd been shot down and had a bad back because of it. He was the only guy there wearing a suit.

Later, on the way home, Sis asked Mom about him. She told us he was a lawyer, but not the same kind as Perry Mason, the television lawyer my parents watched. Mr. Peterson helped people with their wills. Mom said that's something you need when you die. It didn't sound like something I'd want to do.

The two youngest Peterson kids, both of them boys, were too young to be in school yet. Wearing matching tee shirts and shorts, they went inside with their parents carrying identical

24

toy trucks. The two oldest Peterson kids were girls. They both looked older than Sis.

Rena, the oldest one, had on a white sweater and a pleated skirt, which was the latest craze. Her waist was as skinny as a wasp's, and her silver belt buckle was as big as a paperback book. She and her sister, Peggy, both had shoulder length light brown hair. Rena's was pulled back and held with a white plastic hair band. Peggy's hair was loose. Her tan colored slacks and brownish madras blouse looked nice together.

Even though Sis hadn't seen them since last year, it didn't stop them from acting like best friends who saw each other every day. And before long the gossip started with Rena droning on about some guy she wanted to marry. Even though the guy was an airplane mechanic in the air force, which sounded like a cool job, her dad thought he was no good and wouldn't let her marry the guy. She was telling Sis that they planned to run away when she noticed me watching them. She said something to the other girls and they walked across the yard out of earshot.

That left me with Tommy Lee and Margo, the other Peterson kid, who was just about the prettiest girl I'd ever seen. Her change from the skinny little runt who had looked like a boy last year, into the cutest girl on Earth had to be some kind of voodoo magic. I thought "being under someone's spell" was just one of those dumb things people in the movies said, but it happened to me when I saw Margo. I didn't like the feeling, but I couldn't turn it off. Of course, as much as I enjoyed watching and listening to her, being near her I felt as nervous as the time my teacher made me get up and talk in front of the class.

"Hey, Leonard." It was Tommy Lee. He'd startled me. I'd been hypnotized watching Margo's slow careful movements, as though she was so delicate she might break. But when Tommy Lee said my name it not only jolted me out of my trance, it caused Margo to look my way. She caught me staring at her. I looked away so she wouldn't see me blush.

Because Tommy Lee and I were already sitting in the only chairs on the porch when Margo got there, she sat on the steps. It

25

meant she was facing the yard with her back to us. That's why I'd thought it was safe to stare at her.

Tommy Lee told me to let Margo have my rocker, which I did gladly. I liked the idea of doing something nice for her, thinking that she might like me for it. As we changed places, passing close to each other, she stared right at me, which made me lightheaded.

I took her spot on the porch steps, which meant I had to sit sideways to look at her. Dumb me, that's when I figured out why Tommy Lee told me to let her have my seat – so he'd be sitting next to her and I'd be six feet away facing the wrong direction.

Holding his hand out to her he said, "I'm Tommy Lee."

"Margo," she said, shaking his hand.

It bothered me terribly seeing their hands touch. And not just the touching, but being bothered by it bothered me. I envied the way Tommy Lee talked to Margo without saying anything stupid or leaving awkward silences. Around her my brain seemed to be as slow as molasses and as empty as outer space, and the harder I tried to think of a way to impress Margo, the slower and emptier it got.

When a grinning Tommy Lee pointed at me and told her I was a Yankee, she was nice about it, didn't make any wisecracks about me talking funny. She asked me where I lived. My answer, that I was from New York, seemed to impress her.

I thought I'd gotten one up on Tommy Lee, but then she asked me if I liked living in such a big city.

"Not the city," I said, feeling like a dope.

Tommy Lee told her I got confused easily.

"Do not," I said.

He grinned at me like a schoolyard bully. "You smart mouthing me?"

Hoping I'd sound tougher than I felt, I lowered my voice. "I guess your parents didn't teach you to be nice."

I bet you can guess how that worked out. All puffed up and pleased with himself, Tommy Lee gave me an I-dare-you look. "You wanna make something of it?"

Margo told him to leave me alone. I'm sure she meant well, but it was the worst possible thing she could've done. Of course, Tommy Lee loved it. And why wouldn't he? She'd made it look as though I needed her to protect me, and how could a girl as pretty as Margo ever like a scaredy-cat? And it wasn't the last time Tommy Lee was a bully to me around Margo.

While I waited for Mom to leave I picked loose paint flakes off of Grandad's stairs so I wouldn't have to look Tommy Lee or Margo in the eye, all the time wishing I had a hole to crawl in, and wishing Mom would hurry up. When I ran out of paint chips to pry off I studied my shoes. A million years went by before the Petersons came out with their little boys in tow, and I'd been listening to Tommy and Margo talking the whole time.

Mrs. Peterson told us they had just stopped by to say hello and couldn't stay. When Margo stood up to leave I stood up too. I wasn't going to stay out there by myself with Tommy Lee. But before I could go inside to pressure Mother to leave, Margo's eyes met mine and I froze. She walked right past me, smiling at me as she did, her hand brushing against mine, soft as a falling leaf. I didn't think it was an accident, but I was an idiot when it came to girls. And then she was gone and I hated myself for being too braindead to talk to her, and too slow-witted and scared to stand up to Tommy Lee.

With Margo gone everything changed. Tommy Lee still looked smug, but otherwise he ignored me and read his magazine. I went inside and listened to the old people until Mom was ready to leave.

In the car on the way back to Helen's I asked Mom if Margo was my cousin.

"No."

"So we're not related?"

"No, why?"

Sis looked at me funny, as though she'd just figured something out. "You and Margo were pretty chummy."

"Were not."

"I saw the way she smiled at you."

If Tommy Lee hadn't made a fool of me in front of Margo that would've been the best thing I'd ever heard. Sure, Margo had been friendly when she told Tommy Lee goodbye but she didn't smile at him, and she didn't touch his hand. The thought of her hand touching mine made me giddy.

Too bad the only way I could fix things was to stand up to Tommy Lee in front of Margo. Every time I thought of Margo, Tommy Lee's words came back like a toothache to remind me that I'd chickened out in front of her. The only thing that would be worse was if I got a second chance and chickened out a second time.

WHAT DO I DO ABOUT MARGO

As long as I was busy with my cousins during the day I could pretend the disaster with Margo and Tommy Lee had never happened. But when I settled in at night my brain was free to punish me for being a scaredy-cat, and sure enough it brought up an image of Tommy Lee grinning at me. Behind him I saw Margo's face smiling at me. I wanted to talk to somebody about it. "Hey Tripp."

"Yeah."

"You ever have a girlfriend?"

He mumbled the word, "Nah," just before he started snoring.

To get my mind off Margo, I thought about sneaking out to the lake. It was still at least a day away and no more solid than a cloud, no more real than the idea of infinity, a word my dad had once wasted precious play time explaining to me.

I might have fallen asleep thinking about going to the lake, but the image of Margo smiling at me popped into my head again. That left me feeling happy, which made as much sense as an Eskimo buying a lawnmower. I mean, how can just thinking about someone make me feel good when I'd been horribly embarrassed in front of her? And why daydream about Margo when I could daydream about going fishing with Grandpa Dawson, or riding in a new Corvette, or even being an astronaut?

29

And suppose I did see her again, would my stupid shyness stop me from talking to her? Would Tommy Lee be there to make a fool of me? Those two questions kept me awake.

Next morning during breakfast Sis asked Aunt Helen if she could use their piano to practice. Sis could play fancy classical music not even my mom could play, and Mom was a pretty good piano player. I hadn't heard much classical music before Sis started taking lessons. But since then I'd heard every one of her pieces a million times, and that was enough classical junk for a lifetime.

When we were done eating Sis went to their family room to play the piano. Aunt Helen told Tripp to cut the grass. I offered to help, told him I'd be out in a couple minutes, and that we could take turns. As soon as he went outside I went to find Sis. She was flipping through a music book looking for something. When she saw me her hand froze mid-page long enough to call me a pest before she went back to flipping pages.

Sis was the only person I could talk to about Margo, but first I had to work up the courage, because I'd never talked to anyone about a girl before, had never even imagined I'd like one. Sis asked me what I wanted.

I took a deep breath. "Margo looked at me really hard, like she was trying to see inside my head."

Sis turned around on the piano bench to face me. I knew from her smart-alecky grin that she was going to make a wise-crack about it. I felt the heat of a blush and spun around to leave.

"Wait a minute, Leonard."

Poor me, I was so desperate to know if Margo liked me that I was willing to let Sis pick on me, but I stopped at the door anyway, to see what she had to say.

What she had to say was, "You can be such a dummy."

"Same to you, and double too."

"No, silly," she said, rolling her eyes, "I meant you're a dummy because you can't see that she likes you."

I went back in. Standing by the piano so we could talk quietly in case one of our cousins came to use the bathroom, which was right next door. I asked her what I should do about Margo.

"If you like her tell her so, but don't make a big deal about it. Say it casually, as though you're just stating a fact, like, 'Blue's my favorite color.'"

I shook my head, told her that was never going to happen. First she frowned then she smiled, so I braced myself for a wisecrack. She told me to send Margo a card. After giving it a little thought I actually liked the idea. I'd never get up the courage to tell Margo to her face that I liked her, and this way I didn't have to. I'd never tell her so, but Sis always had been the smart one.

My excitement was short lived when I realized that I had a problem. "Where am I gonna get a card?"

"At the Hallmark store, silly."

I told her, "No thanks" then left.

She called me back, asked, "Why's that a problem?"

"I'd have to ask Mom to take me there."

"So?"

"So she'd give me the third degree, and sure as shooting, before long she'd figure out that I liked Margo."

"So?"

"You don't get it do you, Sis?"

"I guess not."

I left then because the last thing in the world I wanted to do was talk to my mom about Margo. I didn't help Tripp with the lawn. I was too depressed to do anything with anyone, so I sat on the back door stoop by myself and watched Mattie. She was sitting by herself in the grass a few feet away playing with a doll that had seen better days. Its clothes were covered with sand and its hair was tangled with twigs. She had it lying in the grass in front of her and she was shaking a finger at it. "You've been a very naughty girl."

Then she held the doll up to her face and shook it. "You're trying my patience, young lady."

Turning it over, she gave it a slap on the butt. "Don't ever

31

do that again."

Mattie noticed me watching her. She made a face then got up and took her doll out near the fence where she sat in the grass facing away from me. I supposed she was replaying a time when she'd gotten into trouble. Only Mattie knew the answer to that and she wasn't talking.

So there I sat, doing nothing, until I saw a big fat rain drop go splat on the steps near my feet, then another one, then a few more. Pretty soon the real rain started and the door behind me popped open. Aunt Helen yelled, "You kids get in here before you get soaked."

Mattie was the last one in. Aunt Helen gave her a slap on the butt, asked her, "Y'all couldn't tell it was raining?" Instead of a slap on the butt, Aunt Helen said to me, "I declare, Lainard, I thought you had more sense than that."

"WE'RE GOING TONIGHT."

The rain didn't last long and just made the humidity worse. That evening when we were outside I got so sweaty that Tripp's grass cuttings stuck to my arms when we laid in the grass; so hot that sweat dripped off my forehead into my eyes, stinging them.

Uncle Bud let Tripp set up the lawn sprinkler for us, and Aunt Helen gave us a pile of towels. Sis went inside to practice the piano so she wouldn't have to run through the sprinkler, something I'd never seen her doing back home. Of course, she never got sweaty like me either.

Leigh wore a bathing suit. Tripp and Mattie and I all wore shorts. Dana ran alongside whoever was going through the sprinkler, always staying just beyond the reach of the water. When Uncle Bud told us we had to shut the sprinkler off so we wouldn't run the well dry we chased fireflies. But that didn't last long because we got hot again.

Tripp turned on the hose so we could drink from it, and while we stood around in a circle flapping our towels to shoo the horse flies away and taking turns drinking, Leigh made a big announcement. "We're going tonight while the moon's full."

In just a few hours I'd be going on my biggest adventure ever. Thrilled by the thought, when I wasn't worried about getting caught, I asked Leigh if the fishing was better when the moon was full.

"No silly, we're going tonight so we won't need flashlights."

Leigh told Tripp to get worms for fish bait. He went to the shed and came back with an old beat up coffee can and a shovel, which he and I used to dig for night crawlers out by the pasture fence, taking turns digging then sifting through the dirt clods with our fingers for worms. When the can was half full with a writhing mass of worms Tripp capped it with a flat rock then hid it in the weeds by the fence.

We were washing the dirt and sweat off our hands with the garden hose when Aunt Helen stuck her head out the back door and yelled, "It's high time you kids came in."

After brushing our teeth and changing into our pajamas Tripp and I got into bed to wait for Aunt Helen to come tell us goodnight. When she left and we saw the hall light under our bedroom door go out we changed back into the clothes we'd worn that day then lay down to wait for Leigh.

I daydreamed about catching a fish as big as me, a fish so big it almost capsized the boat, so big Margo read about it in the newspaper. I let that thought go because it had gotten too silly, even for me. Then I remembered the time Margo's hand had brushed against mine and wondered if she felt the same tingling I did. Then Tommy Lee popped into my head to ruin my daydream.

Forever went by before Leigh cracked our door open and whispered, "Come on, y'all."

Sis and Mattie were waiting in the hallway with Leigh. The five of us tiptoed through the house in our stocking feet, grabbing our shoes as we went through the mudroom then sitting outside on the stoop to put them on.

The Ritcheys had a little wooden footbridge in their backyard. Not much longer or wider than the cot I slept on, it was too narrow for more than one person to walk across at a time. Uncle Bud built it to keep my cousins safe from the blacksnakes that sometimes hid in the tall grass growing in the drainage ditch under it. That night it felt like crossing a magic bridge, because on the other side we passed through some bushes that made us invisible to Aunt Helen and Uncle Bud. That's when the adventure really began.

At the edge of their yard we came to the first of several barbed wire fences we'd have to get past that night. Taking a running start Leigh vaulted it, clearing it easily by pushing off a fencepost. She stood in the pasture on the other side waiting for us. That was the first of many times she said, "Hurry up, y'all," that night.

I got over the fence by holding onto the fencepost for balance while I climbed the wires then jumped down on the other side. Tripp vaulted over the fence, not as easily as Leigh had, but he made it. After imagining getting tangled in the sharp wire, I wondered if I dared to jump the next fence.

Tripp pulled up on the bottom strand of barbed wire for Mattie who'd been standing there with her hands on her hips looking quite impatient in a very grown up sort of way. She rolled under the fence, brushing the dirt off her bare knees when she stood up then skipping on ahead with pine needles stuck to the back of her dress. Tripp held the two top wires apart for Sis then hurried to catch up with Mattie so he could brush the pine needles off.

As we walked through the first of several pastures Dana came out of the dark at a dead run, racing past us, almost to the end of the pasture before turning around to race back to within twenty feet of us. He walked with us after that.

He went to Leigh first, letting let her pet him once. He did the same with Tripp. Then he waited for Mattie to catch up with him. She pet him a few times. When she stopped he pushed his nose up under her hand until she petted him some more.

After they'd played that game half a dozen times, he looked at me, deciding whether or not to let me pet him, I suppose. His answer: he barked at me then ran out ahead of us. When we stopped to climb over the next fence Dana ran to a gate at the far end of the pasture where he squeezed through an opening between the gate and the fence post then ran back to join us. My dog would never do anything like that. Was she friendly enough? You bet. Was she smart enough? Nope, she was as dumb as a fence post.

TROUBLE AT THE LAKE

Mattie sometimes stopped for no reason, at least not one that I could see. But Tripp always stayed back with her, coaxing her along and yelling to Leigh to wait for them.

Having none of that, Leigh would yell back, "If you ever want to come out with us again, Mattie, you'd better hurry up."

Then Mattie would walk a little faster. She and Tripp would still fall behind, just not as quickly. I walked most of the way by myself, which was kind of spooky because the rows of tall pines that marked the boundaries of their pastures made jagged black lines against the moonlit sky and cast long eerie moon shadows across the prairie. And the ancient-looking live oak trees draped with Spanish moss that looked like witch's hair didn't help.

It already seemed like a perilous journey into the unknown, even before I heard the howl of a coyote somewhere far off in the night. It raised the hairs on my neck. I had only ever heard them on television. Looking in the direction of the coyote call instead of where I was walking, I bumped into Dana. He had stopped and was staring toward the sound.

He didn't move a muscle until Leigh told him, "Get it, Dana." Then he took off at a dead run, disappearing into the woods. A few minutes later he came racing back. After barking at us several times, telling us about his daring exploit I suppose,

37

he ran out ahead again until he was as far away as I could throw a stone. When he came back he walked up to Mattie and nudged her hand with his nose. She knelt down and gave him a hug. He licked her face.

"Ew, Mattie," Leigh said, "don't let him do that."

So naturally Mattie put her face near his mouth for him to lick, and naturally Dana licked it. Tripp grabbed her hand and gave it yank to get her walking. Dana trotted alongside her.

I dropped back to ask Tripp how often he went fishing at the lake.

"Never."

"Then how do you know there's fish in the lake?"

"Guys pay my dad to fish there."

"How big are they?"

He shrugged his shoulders, said he didn't know. I bet him I'd catch a bigger fish than him.

"What's the bet?"

"Loser has to kiss the other guy's fish."

"Okay, let's spit on it?"

We stopped, spit on our hands then shook on it, which made it life and death sacred. After that we crossed two more pastures and climbed over two more fences, and each time we waited for Mattie and Tripp to catch up, and each time Leigh threatened to leave Mattie at home the next time she ventured out.

And then I saw the thing they called a lake, a gigantic black jewel shimmering in the moonlight. A sinister-looking expanse of dark water that stretched so far into forever I couldn't find the line between it and the night sky.

And if that wasn't scary enough, it wasn't really a lake. It was a swamp, no doubt in my mind. Clumps of reeds lined the shore. Beyond that, for about fifty feet out from shore, the water was covered with scummy stuff that glowed a puke-green color in the moonlight, not something I'd want to swallow if I fell in.

Out beyond that, moonlight sparkled off silver waves in the pitch black water. It looked like the kind of place where evil things lurked, waiting for some kids like us to come along and be their dinner. It was a lot scarier than anything I'd seen in the monster movies I liked to watch, and this was real.

Then I had a thought so frightening it took my breath away. What if there were alligators in there? So, yeah, I was scared, and plenty. But no matter how scared I got, I couldn't let my cousins know.

When I was a kid I had a picture book showing fishermen at work. I had imagined that my cousin's boat would look like the one in that book, but the wreck of a rowboat lying face down in the weeds near the shore looked as though I could smash it to bits with one good kick.

And as if that wasn't bad enough, Tripp told us to stay where we were, that, "There might be a rattlesnake under the boat."

Tearing a clump of mud out of the bank near the waterline he threw it at the boat. It hit with a thud. He waited a few moments before flipping the boat over, jumping back from it as he did.

Leigh sat in the moss near the waterline. "Y'all had better take your shoes and socks off. If we get them wet they'll smell like the lake and Momma will know we were here."

Leigh and Tripp rolled up their pant legs and waded into the water, pulling the boat with them until the water was up to their knees. They backed it up to the shore then held it steady for Sis then Mattie then me so we could get in without getting our feet wet.

I heard Dana whimper when Mattie got in the boat. Leigh and Tripp got in last from opposite sides at the same time so they wouldn't tip the boat over. Tripp took the oars, using one of them to push us away from shore. Mattie waved to Dana. He barked at the sky one time then sat down and whimpered as he watched us leave.

So amid the din of a million crickets, the drone of a far-off gasoline engine, and the occasional croak of a startled frog, our adventure began with us gliding away from the dank-smelling shore, cutting a v-shaped path thorough green swamp scum.

Tripp rowed us out past the scum, into the expanse of inky black water where a beam of sparkling moonlight reflected off the silvery waves. As we inched further out into the lake I wondered what kind of fish were in there and how big they got.

Then an unexpected cold dampness brought my attention back to the boat. My feet were in several inches of water, water than hadn't been there when we got into the boat. I told Leigh about it.

She told Sis, "If y'all don't start bailing we're gonna sink, and I know y'all don't want to be gator bait."

Seeing the panic on Sis's face when she said, "You didn't tell us you had a leaky boat," was almost worth going for a swim with the gators.

Leigh grinned, said, "We don't."

"What do you call that?" Sis said, pointing at the water around our feet, the panic in the voice as clear as day.

"Leigh grinned at her, said, "It's not our boat. It was left here by some guy hunting alligators. I guess he got tired of bailing."

"Now you tell us."

"That's why we brought an empty can."

Sis mumbled something then started bailing. I thought about sinking and what was lurking in the black depths under our boat. I pointed down at the water, asked Leigh, "You were just kidding about the gators, weren't you?"

With a big grin she assured me that there were indeed alligators in their lake, adding, "Dad saw a twelve-footer once."

A few minutes later I heard a loud sloshing near the boat. I almost peed myself when Sis shrieked because she was looking at the water right next to the boat. When I leaned over to look I saw a swirling eddy where something had poked the surface then gone back under. "Guys, there's something in there."

"Must be something big," Leigh said, and her saying it without grinning, practically made it a fact.

Our boat was so flimsy an alligator could smash it into

matchsticks with a flick of its tail. I tucked my arms in close to my sides and searched the water. Tripp suggested that it might have been a big fish or even a water moccasin.

Leigh shook her head. "Nope. Definitely a gator."

By then, the smelly black water in the boat was up to our ankles. Did that scare me? You bet, but not as much as Leigh telling Sis, "If you don't bail faster, Sarah, we're gonna sink for sure."

By then Tripp had rowed us so far out into the lake that the trees along the shore looked like a string of little black paper cutouts held against the moonlit sky, the kind you make by cutting folded black paper. If our boat sank it would be a long, slow, terrifying swim back with me all the time expecting an alligator to clamp down on my leg.

I noticed Tripp staring at me. He must've thought I was a real scaredy-cat with my arms pulled up tight against my chest, and my hands in my armpits. So put my hands in my lap and swore no one would see me acting scared the rest of the night, even if something killed me. Then I saw Mattie leaning over the side of the boat, her face inches from the water as she dragged her hand in it, calmly watching the ripples spreading out behind it.

When Leigh saw what she was doing, she told Mattie, "If you don't keep your hand in the boat a gator's gonna bite it right off."

My hand would've been out of there in a blink. But not Mattie. She shrugged her little shoulders then calmly pulled her hand out of the water and wiped it on her dress.

Moments later Leigh told us to hush. Sis asked her why.

"I heard somebody," Leigh said, pointing toward a spot on the shore up ahead. "Over there."

Tripp pulled on the oars to turn the boat around. Leigh asked him what he was doing.

"Heading back."

"Don't you want to know who it is and what they're doing out here in the middle of the night?"

41

"Nope."

"Then give me the oars."

"Nope."

Leigh stood up. "I'll tip the boat over."

Tripp shook his head.

I never for one second thought she'd really do it, but she did, sloshing scummy green water into the boat. If she rocked the boat like that again she'd sink it for sure.

Bailing frantically, Sis begged Leigh to sit down then reminded her that Mattie couldn't swim.

At least I had a chance, but Mattie would drown for sure if the gators didn't get her first. Poor kid should have been terrified. I sure as heck would've been. But Mattie clapped her hands and giggled with delight. And when Tripp handed Leigh the oars Mattie said, "Oh poop."

Leigh told her to shush. I hate being a scaredy-cat, hate anyone knowing I'm a scaredy-cat, but I was so relieved when Tripp chickened out, that I almost clapped my hands. I'd had enough of our big adventure, and I was willing to bet that Sis wished she was back in bed, under her covers with a flashlight reading a book.

Mattie tried to rock the boat by leaning from side to side. When that didn't work she pleaded with Leigh to rock it. Leigh told her to hush. Mattie folded her arms and pouted. Leigh rowed us closer to shore then used the oars to pull the boat into a clump of reeds. I glimpsed two men standing near an old pumper truck, the kind firemen use. A hose as big around as my arm ran down to the lake from the truck. A second one ran from the truck into the woods behind them.

One of the men, a pudgy guy wearing a cowboy hat, was looking in our direction. The other man's face lit up from the pulsing glow of a cigarette.

Sis asked Leigh what they were doing.

"Stealing our water, pumping it into their irrigation ditches."

"How do you know they're stealing it?"

"If they had permission they wouldn't be doing it in the middle of the night."

The man wearing the cowboy hat pointed in our direction. "I hear something over there." He turned a police car type spotlight attached to the truck toward us. A flash of light nearly blinded me.

Leigh handed the oars to Tripp. "Here, take 'em. You're a lot stronger than I am"

"You wanted them so bad, you do it."

"They might be the same men Uncle Pete caught stealing water a few years back. He said they were dangerous. So you'd better take the oars and get us out of here."

Pointing at us, one of the men yelled, "Come on, they're over that way."

THE OGRE'S PLACE

Tripp pulled on the oars so hard his butt came up off the seat. Sitting in the bow, Leigh paddled with both hands. Although I imagined a three-foot-long snout bristling with teeth clamping down on my arm, I reached into the water with my left hand to paddle. I was more afraid of men I could see than an alligator I couldn't. But, between watching the shore for the men, and watching the water rise around my ankles, I don't think I was much help.

Sis stopped bailing to help paddle. She even put her hands in the slimy swamp water. Mattie paddled too, although mostly she splashed water on us and giggled a lot. So it was all on Tripp to get us out of there.

After Tripp rammed the boat onto the shore we scrambled out then sat in the grass and struggled to pull our socks on over our wet feet, all of us except Mattie whose rubber boots had kept her feet dry. In spite of my trembling fingers and a wary eye on the nearby woods I got my left shoe on and tied, and my right sock on. While I fumbled with the laces on my right shoe, I heard rustling in the bushes behind us.

Leigh whispered, "Hurry up," just before a man burst out of the trees with another man a few feet behind him. They ran at us. We scattered. One of them lunged at Mattie. She spun and twisted like a scared rabbit. The man got a handful of her dress. She struggled, but he held on, lifting her off the ground with one hand. She kicked his legs ferociously. He hardly noticed. She screamed, a high-pitched, ear-punishing squeal. He noticed that.

44

It distracted him. Seeing her chance, Leigh charged him. He saw her coming and shoved her, hard. After landing on her butt, she got up and moved to his right. Tripp moved to his left. I moved in between my cousins.

The one holding Mattie asked the other one, "What do you think I should do with the brat?"

Leigh told him he'd better let her go. He made a show of spitting then laughed at her. I was shaking in my shoes. I didn't think things could look any worse when I heard more noises coming from the bushes behind us, but louder this time. It had to be something big. The way the bushes were shaking you'd have thought it was an elephant.

A mangy-looking, long-haired, bearded man burst out of the bushes at a dead run headed straight for Mattie. The man holding her dropped her, raising his hands in self-defense. The wild man crashed into him so hard he knocked the guy clean off his feet. Mattie scurried away while the two men wrestled in the grass.

Tripp picked Mattie up with one arm and ran, staying near the lakeshore, with Sis and Leigh and me scrambling after him. When I was far enough away to feel safe, I stopped to look back. I saw three men fighting. If anyone was winning I couldn't tell who, and I didn't stay to watch.

I ran hard to catch up with the others. Sis with her long legs had kept up with Leigh. Fortunately, Tripp had stopped to wait for us. When I caught up with them I looked back again. This time I saw two men lying on the ground, neither of them moving.

Lee pointed at some trees, said, "I saw the wild man go that way" then walked off in that direction.

Sis told her we should hurry home, and, "We need to tell your parents what happened."

Leigh stopped and turned around to face her. "Y'all can go home if you want," then she headed off.

Tripp and Sis and I looked at each other. I hoped one of them would head home so I could follow them without looking like a scaredy-cat. But Mattie put the kibosh on that when she grabbed Sis's hand then Tripp's, pulling them in the direction Leigh had gone. It was follow them or wander around the prairie in the dark by myself looking for my cousins' house. I ran after them in my squishy wet socks and sneakers.

Leigh stopped near a clump of trees to wait for us. I asked her who she thought the wild man was. She shrugged her shoulders.

Mattie declared that, "He's an ogre," with the certainty of a child who still believes in fairytales.

Leigh rolled her eyes. "There's no such a thing as ogres, Mattie."

Mattie crossed her arms over her little chest. "Are so, aren't there, Aunt Sarah."

That got a smile from Sis. "I'm your cousin, Mattie, not your aunt."

"But you're almost as old as my Aunt Lilly."

"Doesn't matter. I'm still your cousin."

Mattie frowned then walked after Leigh with her little shoulders slumped so far over she looked like a cartoon character. Being corrected by Sis must have been super embarrassing for her. Tripp went after Mattie. We caught up with Leigh a few moments later. She was looking intently at a light in the distance. I asked her what it was.

"Our great-granddaddy's cabin."

I asked her why her he lived way out there.

"He doesn't. He died a long time ago."

"Then who lives there?"

"I think it's the guy who saved our butts at the lake."

Tripp asked Leigh, "You're going over there, aren't you?"

"Yep."

Tripp told her it was a bad idea. "He's probably a squatter, and Dad says they're dangerous."

Leigh called him a wuss then headed for the cabin.

Muttering something under his breath Tripp took Mattie by the hand and followed Leigh. Sis followed them. I did not want to meet the wild man from the lake, even if he did save our butts. But what choice did I have?

When she got to the cabin Leigh crouched next to a side wall near the front porch, where she'd be out of sight of anyone inside. The place looked like two sheds connected by a covered walkway, which I learned later was called a dogtrot. Each of the sheds was about the size of my bedroom back home. The light we'd seen was coming from a window with a torn curtain.

I think I could've blown the place down. The sagging roof over the walkway had partially fallen in, leaving a gaping hole open to the stars, and neither of the windows I could see had glass in them. Except for Sis and her long legs, the step up onto the floor of the dogtrot, which was knee-high, would be tough because the stairs had rotted and caved in.

And it looked as though the whole cabin would soon get swallowed up by the Palmetto bushes around it. The cabin, the trees with their streamers of gray moss hanging over it, and the feeble light leaking out through the torn curtain illuminating jumbled patches of branches and leaves, looked like one of those really hard thousand-piece jigsaw puzzles.

Leaning in close, Tripp whispered to me. "Watch this. Leigh'll do anything on a dare. Hey Leigh."

"What?"

"I double-dog dare you to knock on the door."

She grinned then walked around to the front of the dogtrot, and pivoting off her left hand, which she'd placed on the floor of the dogtrot, leapt up onto it, making it look easy. After walking up to the door without a moment's hesitation, she looked around at us with a grin and told us, "Y'all are a bunch of pansies" then knocked on the door.

When no one answered, Tripp told Sis and me, "Watch out for snakes" then climbed up onto the dog trot and held his hand out for Mattie. Her tiny hand disappeared inside his as he lifted her up onto the dogtrot as easily as I'd lift one of her dolls.

That left Sis and me. Sis made a face then stepped up onto the dog trot. No way was I staying outside by myself in the dark, especially if there might be snakes around. I climbed up to join the others.

By then Leigh had opened the door and gone inside. I peeked in the doorway. The light we'd seen was coming from one of those old railroad-type kerosene lanterns sitting on an overturned wooden crate in the far corner of the room.

The crate, which had a partially-used pack of matches on it, was next to a mattress on the floor that had no blanket or sheet on it. The pillow was too dirty looking even for me to put my head on. Except for a shoe box on the floor next to the mattress, and a small framed picture of Jesus hanging on the wall, there wasn't another thing in the room. So many pages from old newspapers and magazines had been glued to the walls, to keep the cold out I suppose, that it looked like some kid's paper mache school project.

Leigh was standing next to the crate, which had fragments of what looked like an old advertisement for Georgia peaches stuck to it. She picked up the shoebox and began sifting through the stuff inside. I couldn't imagine what was in there and didn't much care. I just hoped we'd be gone before the owner came back, especially if it was the wild man we'd seen at the lake.

Leigh spun around suddenly, the unexpected motion startling me so badly my heart skipped a beat. She held up a pink plastic kid's flute. "Remember this, Mattie?"

Mattie grabbed for it, yelling, "Hey, that's mine."

Leigh held it higher. Mattie jumped for it. Leigh kept it just out of her reach. Mattie made an angry face and stomped her foot. I told Leigh I thought we should go.

When she said, "Y'all can go but I'm waiting here until he gets back," my heart sank.

Bang. Coming from behind me, the loud noise had scared me so badly I'd almost jumped out of my shoes.

CAUGHT BY THE OGRE

The wild man from the lake stood in the doorway. He had pushed the door to the dogtrot open so hard it had slammed into the wall. He sure did look scary, his eyes looking around panicky-like in the lantern's light, the way I imagined the eyes of a trapped, crazed killer would look. His wiry gray eyebrows looked like smoke caught in a gust of wind. And his long, tangled, madman hair looked as though he'd just come in out of a wind storm.

His pants were badly stained, and even though it was a hot summer night he had on a torn and crumpled long-sleeved shirt. I saw a dark spot on his lip where a trickle of blood had dried and a darkness around his left eye that looked like the start of a shiner.

Saying, "Sweet Jesus," Tripp backed away from the guy pulling Mattie back with him. His face had that scrunched up, "I think I'm going to get hurt" look, like the kid who realizes he shouldn't have poked the schoolyard bully.

Sis took a step back from the guy. I did too, so I wouldn't be closer to him than her. Not Leigh; she and Wild Man eyed each other like two school kids having a stare-down.

Mattie whispered, "See, I told you he's an ogre,' loud enough for the guy to hear.

Wild Man yelled, "Put that back."

I cringed.

"Who are you?" Leigh asked,

"Amu," was all he said, in a voice as deep as a well. Then he pointed at the toy flute Leigh was holding. "Put it back."

Leigh put it back in the shoe box then set the box on the floor. "Sure, mister, but you shouldn't be here."

He pointed at Sis, asked Leigh, "What's she doing here?"

Leigh looked startled. I know I was. Who'd he think my sister was anyway?

He asked Leigh, "Is that your Mom?"

"She's my cousin."

Then he looked at Mattie. At first he tipped his head and looked confused. Then he smiled at her. He didn't smile at anyone else, just asked what we were doing at the swamp.

"Fishing."

He shook his head and kept shaking it while he said, "There's bad things in there."

Tripp told him we had a boat.

"That boat won't save you."

That was all I needed to hear. I was never going out on that lake again, especially not in that boat.

"Save us from what?" Leigh asked.

He didn't answer.

She asked him, "You're the guy who helped us at the lake, aren't you?"

He took out a knife, and not your typical Boy Scout jackknife. This one had a blade as long as a new pencil, and it scared the bejesus out of me. He knelt down in front of Mattie. It happened so fast, and had been so unexpected that not one of us did anything to help her.

"There's evil in that swamp," Amu said, taking off the necklace he was wearing, a ratty-looking jumble of trash, the kind of stuff you see at the seashore after a storm. He cut the string in two places then knelt down and tied one of the pieces around Mattie's neck.

He told her, "This'll keep you safe, but don't ever take it off. If you do you'll break the spell."

With a big dramatic nod of her head Mattie promised to

wear it forever. Amu mumbled some strange-sounding stuff in another language.

Leigh told him, "She doesn't need your foolishness, mister. She's foolish enough already."

"Am not," Mattie said, at the same time Amu said, "Ain't nothing foolish about it."

Leigh sneered. "That's just some junk on a shoelace."

Amu pulled his shirt up and showed us his chest. Then he turned around so we could see his back. "Does this look like foolishness?"

At first I thought he had a costume on under his shirt, because I saw long, puckered, whitish lumps running every which way across his front and back, as though a bunch of snakes had crawled under his skin then shriveled up and died. I wondered what could have done that to him, wondered what it had felt like.

He put his shirt down. "Croc did that to me, had me in a death grip, rolling me over and over in the mud, and me trying to gouge his eyes out the whole time. Lucky for me he caught me in a shallow spot. If he'd 'a caught me in deeper water he would've pulled me under. That's how they kill you, you know. They pull you under and drown you before they eat you."

He held up the other half of the necklace. "This here charm's what saved me."

I wouldn't have argued with such a scary guy, but then I wasn't Leigh. "Mister," she said, pointing at the necklace, "if a croc got hold of you, you'd be as dead as the bird you took the bones from for your necklace."

"I'm the one who was eye to eye with that devil, and damned if I didn't dig one of his eyes. That's when he stopped fighting and swam away. And he's been looking to get even with me ever since."

Leigh shook her head. "Never happen, mister. Besides, all the crocs are down south. It gets too cold for them up here."

Tripp told Leigh we'd be late getting home if we didn't get going.

51

Amu gave us a quick, worried glance. "You won't tell anyone you seen me, will ya?"

Leigh shook her head. "No, mister, I reckon we won't. But if you stay here, someone's gonna find you, just as sure as we're standing here."

Amu stepped away from the door, giving us room to get past him. I felt my muscles relax all over my body, felt my breathing slow almost back to normal. Tripp took Mattie by the hand and led her out.

Leigh followed them but stopped when she was face to face with Amu. "Thanks for helping at the lake."

"You kids stay away from that swamp."

I hurried past him, out onto the dogtrot then leapt off the porch sailing past Tripp who was helping Mattie down.

When we were a stone's throw from the cabin Amu yelled to us. "I can't help you if that croc comes after you."

I looked back, saw Amu standing in the dogtrot, his black shape and wild man hair outlined in the light from the doorway.

"CAN YOU KEEP A SECRET?"

It wasn't long before Leigh got far out ahead of us again and Tripp yelled for her to wait.

When Sis and I caught up with her, Leigh told Sis, "I don't think he liked you."

"I wonder why. And why was he nice to Mattie after she called him an ogre?"

"Yeah, that was weird."

Sis asked Leigh if Amu could've gotten his scars from an alligator.

"Not and live to tell about it."

By then Tripp and Mattie had joined us.

Sis told Mattie, "You shouldn't call him an ogre."

Mattie crossed her arms over her chest and pouted, and asked Sis, "Oh yeah? How come?".

"How would you like it, Mattie, if the kids at school called you ugly?"

"They don't."

"Well we should judge people by what they do, not how they look. Amu didn't have to save us from those two men at the lake, but he did and we should be grateful. I'm sorry I didn't thank him. "

The awkward silence that followed was broken by Leigh who held her hand out to Mattie. "Let me see the necklace."

When Mattie told her, "no," Leigh grabbed for it.

Mattie twisted away. "It's mine," she said, clutching it, "and you can't have it."

"Yeah okay, you win."

Mattie held the necklace up to look at it without taking it off. While she was busy studying it Leigh bent down to pick up something on the ground by Mattie's feet. As she stood up she snatched the necklace from Mattie, pulling it up over her head. Mattie grabbed for it but missed. Leigh held it up over her head. Mattie jumped for it and almost got it. Leigh held it higher.

Holding the necklace up in the moonlight to inspect it, Leigh fingered the pieces on the string. "This might be a baby alligator's tooth and these bones are small and hollow like a bird's bones."

Tripp said, "I bet it's some kind of voodoo."

Leigh said, "Nah, it's just some old junk on a string."

Mattie yelled, "Give it back."

Leigh grinned at Mattie then tossed the necklace over her head to Tripp. The meltdown started with a quivering bottom lip and glistening eyes. Sis held her hand out to Tripp. He gave her the necklace. She gave it to Mattie.

With a tear rolling down her cheek, Mattie uttered a feeble, "Thank you, Aunt Sarah."

Sis didn't correct her that time.

Then stabbing the air angrily, Mattie pointed her index finger at her sister. "You ruined it."

"Yeah? What'd I ruin?"

"The magic," Mattie said, sniffling back her tears.

"There's no such thing as magic; no such things as ogres neither. Now, come on, we have to get home. The sun will be up in an hour or two."

Tripp reached for Mattie's hand. She pulled it away. He grabbed it and held on.

A few minutes later, when we were a stone's throw from the fence at the edge of their back yard, Leigh stopped to wait for us. Sis and I joined her to wait for Mattie and Tripp.

54

When they caught up with us, Leigh said to us, "You gotta promise you won't tell a soul about going to the lake, especially our parents, even if it means getting in trouble. Because if they find out we snuck out to the lake we'll be lucky if they just whup us with a ruler."

Tripp agreed and so did I. A pouty Mattie nodded her head.

Leigh asked Sis, "How about you, Sarah, you promise not to tell?"

"It's not that simple, Leigh."

"Sure it is. You're either with us or you're not."

Sis walked away. We'd have to wait and see if she told Aunt Helen and Uncle Bud what had happened, which meant I wouldn't know until morning if I'd catch hell for it, which meant I wouldn't sleep for crap.

Later, while Tripp and I were putting our pajamas on for bed, I asked him what he thought of Amu.

"Guy's weirder than a three-eyed snake."

"You think he got those scars from a crocodile?"

"Is your sister gonna rat on us?"

"I hope not."

He moaned then rolled over, snoring almost immediately. There wasn't much chance of me doing that after such a scary night. I got the creeps just thinking about the leaky boat, and the swamp, and the two men chasing us, not to mention Amu. He might've saved our butts, but he was still scary.

And I was sleeping someplace I wasn't used to, so every little noise their house made woke me up, and every time it happened I imagined the men from the lake breaking in to get us. But next thing I knew Aunt Helen was shaking me. I sat up and yawned.

She shook Trip's foot. "Wake up sleepyhead."

Tripp complained, even after his mom told us she'd made pancakes and bacon. What kid wouldn't happily jump out of bed for that? So it was no wonder she asked, "What's the matter with y'all?"

There was a sleepy-looking bunch of kids sitting at the

table that morning, and lots of yawning and eye rubbing. Of course we weren't too sleepy to wolf down a mountain of pancakes and a truckload of bacon.

When we'd had our fill, Aunt Helen sat down with us. The way she went around the table, stopping to look at each of us for what seemed like an eternity, made me really anxious. She stopped at Leigh. "You want to tell me why you're all so tired this morning?"

Leigh, who could keep a secret, and was not at all afraid of being punished if that was the price of keeping it, shrugged her shoulders. Aunt Helen asked Tripp if there something he wanted to tell her.

He said, "No ma'am," but without looking at her, which was as good as saying, "Yep, you got me. I'm guilty."

Aunt Helen looked around the table at each of us again, slowly, one at a time, the way parents do when they know you're hiding something. "Y'all have been somewhere you shouldn't have. I can smell it on you."

To avoid her stare I looked down at my empty breakfast plate. It would look like an admission of guilt, but she'd ask me questions if I looked her in the eye, and if she did, somehow I'd goof up and say something I shouldn't, 'cause that's what I do.

As she stood up from the table, she said, "Lord help y'all if I find out you were at the lake."

I shuddered to think how mad she'd be if she found out that we took Mattie out in the boat.

TROUBLE FOR TRIPP

Two days later Tripp took us for a ride on an old hay wagon. His dad had parked it next to the carport and left it hooked up to one of their old farm tractors when he went to town. Aunt Helen had gone to town for groceries. Us kids were hanging around trying to think of something fun to do when Leigh suggested that Tripp take us for a ride on the wagon.

Tripp told her "no" in no uncertain terms, as my Mom would say.

"Come on, Tripp," Leigh said, "it'll be fun."

"It'll be fun for you because I'm the one who'll get the whupping."

"What if I promise not to be mean for a whole month?"

"No, and that's final."

Leigh grinned at Tripp. "You're forcing me to do it."

He winced. "Do what?"

"Tell Mom about the dirty magazine hidden in your closet."

He didn't deny it, didn't say a word actually, so I figured it was probably true.

Mattie tugged on Leigh's shirt sleeve. "Will he really get in trouble for just getting a magazine dirty?"

Leigh snickered, told her, "It's not that kind of dirty."

"Dirt's dirt, ain't it?"

Sis told Mattie she shouldn't say "ain't."

Mattie asked Tripp if she could see the magazine.

Leigh told her no.

"Why not?"

"Because there's nudies in it, that's why."

Mattie made a pouty face. "I wanna see."

Tripp slumped over. He looked utterly dejected. "Nice going, Leigh. Now she'll blab to Mom."

"If you take us for a ride, I'll make her promise not to. If you don't, I'll tell Momma myself."

Poor Tripp groaned then said, "Okay," and that's how we got a ride on the hay wagon.

Leigh knelt down facing Mattie. "Promise me you won't tell."

"I promise I won't tell nobody."

"Anybody," Sis said, "you won't tell anybody."

"That's what I said, Aunt Sarah."

"I'm your cousin, Mattie, not your aunt."

I had a feeling Tripp was going to get whupped in spite of Mattie's promise, because promises are a lot harder to keep than they are to make.

Tripp insisted that one of us run out to the road and watch for his mom and dad. I said I'd do it because I didn't really want a ride on the wagon anyway.

"No," Leigh said, "it's Mattie's turn."

"But I don't want to."

"Too bad."

So Mattie took the first turn, and while she danced and pranced and skipped her way down the driveway toward the road, the rest of us used the tow bar as a step to climb up onto the chest-high wagon platform that had been polished smooth by years of work boots and hay bales.

When Mattie got to the road Tripp started the tractor and the wagon lurched forward. As he pulled us down the circular drive toward the road Mattie twirled like a ballerina several times then skipped around the mailbox with one hand on the post, as though she was at a ball dancing with Prince Charming.

Next time I checked she was squatting on her haunches looking at something in the tall grass. Having her for a lookout spelled doom for poor Tripp. And I was right about riding on the wagon – it wasn't much fun, definitely not worth poor Tripp getting in trouble.

Making the turn back toward the house put Mattie out of sight behind us. The one time I looked back she was still monkeying with something in the grass. Moments later I heard a car door slam and spun around to look.

Aunt Helen had driven up behind us, close enough for me to see the angry look on her face. We hadn't heard the car because of the loud tractor. Mattie was up on her knees in the front seat leaning on the dashboard. Aunt Helen got out of the car and stood there with her fists on her hips waiting for Poor Tripp to park the wagon.

The moment Tripp shut the tractor off she let him have it. "What in God's name were you thinking, leaving Mattie out there on the road by herself?"

"That was Leigh's idea."

"And what's this I hear about a magazine?"

Tripp's body sagged like a marionette with its strings cut.

"And how did Mattie find out about it, Tripp?"

"Leigh told her."

"I suppose you're going to blame her for driving the tractor without permission."

Tripp only got as far as, "But she...," before Aunt Helen grabbed him and spun him around by the arm and swatted his butt. "You get in the house this instant."

Leigh waited for about a minute after her mom and Tripp had gone indoors then snuck inside. Sis and Mattie and I waited nervously outside on the front steps. Well not Mattie, she had taken one of her boots off and was filling it with driveway gravel, counting the stones as she dropped them in.

When Leigh came out a few minutes later to announce, "He got the ruler," she didn't look at all upset. Brothers and sisters, go figure.

THE BLACKSNAKE

Next morning while us kids were lying in the grass out back trying to decide what to do next Mattie caught my eye. After she checked to be sure no one else was looking, she gave me an impish look then picked her nose and threatened to eat what she'd found in there. By the time I got Leigh's attention Mattie had picked a buttercup and asked Sis to join her.

Sis, having played that game before, knelt in the grass while Mattie held the buttercup under her chin to test her for sweetness. Mattie, who was taking the buttercup test very seriously, announced that Sis was indeed sweet because Mattie had seen a yellow glow under her chin. When Leigh told her that it was just reflected sunlight, Mattie stuck her tongue out at her.

Mattie tried my chin next. It was awfully nice of me to sit still for it, although I did lean to the left to block the sunlight. I didn't want Mattie making a fuss about me being sweet.

Saying, "Stupid buttercup," Mattie threw that one away and picked another one then headed toward Leigh. She stopped when she noticed Leigh standing as still as a garden statue. If it wasn't for Dana's angry barking I'd have thought Leigh was playing a trick on Mattie.

Leigh and Mattie were staring at a patch of tall weedy grass growing in the ditch under the bridge. Dana lunged at the grass, his jaws snapping shut with a loud, empty-sounding clack. Mattie screamed. Tripp grabbed Mattie's hand and yanked her up off the grass. Mattie screamed again. Dana lunged again.

The back door slammed shut with a loud bang. I looked. Aunt Helen ran down the steps, yelled, "You kids get in the house." When none of us moved right away, she screamed, "Now" then ran toward us holding a hoe over her head like a mad woman.

Leigh ran for the back door. Sis and I ran after her. Tripp could almost run carrying Mattie. We all stopped on the stoop to watch the excitement. Mattie stopped screaming and started sniveling.

Holding the hoe high overhead. Aunt Helen yelled, "Get it Dana."

A black shape shot out of the grass. Dana jumped. His teeth snapped shut, catching nothing. The snake had missed him. Aunt Helen brought the hoe down, hard. Pieces of snake as big as my arm thrashed in the weeds, like enormous earthworms on some giant's fishhook. Aunt Helen chopped, and kept on chopping until nothing moved.

Then, breathing hard, she leaned on the hoe. Dana had stopped barking and was nosing around in the weeds. In spite of Aunt Helen yelling at him he carried a big piece of the snake away in his mouth. Even with his head held high the end of the thing dragged in the grass behind him.

I had caught plenty of garter and milk snakes back home in New York. The big ones were as long as my leg. But this blacksnake was longer than my sister was tall. Aunt Helen used a shovel to toss the rest of the snake pieces into the pasture. Then she offered to make us Kool-Aid, and nothing's better on a hot day than sweet, icy-cold, Kool-Aid.

On the way in she gave Leigh a hard flat-handed whack on the butt, hard enough to have stung. "When I tell you to get in the house, you do it, young lady."

Even though Sis and I hadn't moved either, and Aunt Helen hadn't swatted us, Leigh didn't complain about the unfairness of it. I felt bad about it, but not bad enough to ask for a swat on my butt.

Snake or no snake, we went back outside after having our

Kool-Aid. A short while later my mother came for a visit. To make sure Sis and I were behaving ourselves. That's what she told us. More likely, she was worried about me misbehaving.

Dana warned us when Mom's car pulled into the driveway. Tripp and I raced to the front yard. Mother was halfway from the car to the front door when we came around the corner of the house. I yelled for her to wait up.

Tripp let me tell her what had happened. "Aunt Helen killed a huge snake, right in the back yard, right where we were playing. Pretty cool, huh?"

She blinked a couple of times then said, "Oh dear," before going inside, with us right behind her.

She confronted Aunt Helen, who was in the kitchen doing food-type stuff. "Buster tells me you killed a snake today."

"Don't worry. Lizbeth, Dana won't let anything get near the kids."

Mom didn't look satisfied with that. Maybe she thought all dogs were scaredy cats because our dog was such a chicken.

I told her, "You should've seen Aunt Helen chop it up."

"Now Lainard," Aunt Helen said, "that snake wasn't much over six feet."

At that, Mom's face turned three shades of white. She said, "Oh Helen" then grabbed the back of a chair to steady herself.

"You grew up here, Lizbeth. You know how big the snakes get."

"We grew up in town, Helen."

"Oh, that reminds me, Lizbeth, I simply must tell you about the snake I killed last month."

"You're not helping."

After wiping her hands on a towel she waved one at Mom dismissively then turned to face us kids. "I went out one morning to get the mail. It was one of those lazy days when I still had my bathrobe on after breakfast. Of course, that doesn't happen very often these days, what with the kids being home from school for the summer.

"Anyway, Tripp had had a fever of one hundred and four

the night before, so I'd been on the phone all morning talking to Doctor Harrison. You remember Doctor Harrison. He's the one who talks a mile a minute. I swear I can't get a word in edgewise. You'd think he'd have to take a breath once in a while. I do wonder how that man gets any doctoring done."

Mother told Aunt Helen to get to the point, which made Leigh snicker.

"Oh dear. There I go again, getting sidetracked. I swear, it must be old age creeping up on me. I feel fine but, well you never know."

Mom said, "No Helen, I don't," which threw Aunt Helen for a loop, but only for a moment before she was back to telling her story. "When I got to the mailbox I saw a snake curled up in the grass around the post. If I hadn't been paying attention I would've stepped right on it."

Mom asked, "What if one of the kids had gone to get the mail?"

I asked her what she did.

"I ran back to the house and got your Uncle Bud's old service revolver. Damn thing's nearly as big as me, and that's God's truth."

Aunt Helen realized she'd used the Lord's name in vain. She seemed so embarrassed about swearing in front of us kids that I had to stifle the urge to giggle. I noticed that Leigh and Tripp were also trying mightily not to laugh.

Aunt Helen held her hand over her mouth, as though she was telling us a secret, "Y'all pardon my French." Then she went back to her story without missing a beat. "Well, I marched right back out to the mailbox in my bathrobe and shot that snake until the gun was empty."

Mother shook her head. "Helen, if you thought telling me that story would make me feel better, you are sadley mistaken."

"But Lizbeth, I was just getting to the good part."

Not even an angry look from Mom could keep Aunt Helen from finishing her story. "So there I was standing on the side of the road with nothing on but a bathrobe. And didn't the

Wheelers decide to drive by just then? They live up the road a piece. I don't think you knew them. They came to town after you moved up North. They're not what you'd call devout Christians, but I don't suppose the Lord would want me to hold that against them."

Mom asked her to get to the point.

Aunt Helen winced. I don't think she was done telling us about the Wheelers, but she skipped past them and went ahead with her story. "Well alright, but what do you suppose the Wheelers thought when they saw me standing on the side of the road in my bathrobe shooting at my mailbox?"

All of us kids laughed, even Mattie, although I think she only laughed so she wouldn't feel left out.

I knew from the way my mom said, "I'm glad you can make light of it," that she didn't think it was funny.

After that, Mom and Aunt Helen did cooking stuff together. For a while Aunt Helen did all of the talking, with Mother joining in gradually, as she got over the snake, I suppose. Soon they were both talking non-stop. They could do that; talk and listen at the same time. I couldn't possibly do that, but it seemed as natural as breathing for them.

As she went through the hallway door Leigh waved her arm in the air like a sheriff in a TV western taking a posse after the bad guys. "Come on y'all." We followed her to the playroom at the back of the house to play pool on their kid-sized pool table. But poor Mattie, even standing on the bathroom stool she was too short to play.

When Leigh suggested that she color instead she pouted. "I don't have anything to color."

"Momma got you a new coloring book last week."

"I did them."

"All of them?"

"Uh huh."

"You couldn't have."

"Could too," she said, holding up a coloring book and flipping through the pages. "See."

It didn't look as though she'd spent more than a second on any of them. Some of them only had one slash of a single color across the page. Sis offered to draw new pictures for her, which was not at all like my sister. Leigh got them a pile of scrap paper.

Sis drew whatever Mattie asked for, and to my great surprise, did a pretty good job of it. As Mattie colored them in Sis made a big deal about how good they looked. Although they didn't look much better than the ones in the coloring book, Mattie gobbled up the attention.

FEEDING THE CATTLE

Next day when Uncle Bud came back for lunch, we had hamburgers. My cousins had nagged Aunt Helen for them until she gave in. When he was done eating Uncle Bud patted his leg. Mattie climbed up on his lap. Well she didn't exactly climb up. It was more like she leaned against his leg and he scooped her up.

He asked her what she'd been doing then listened patiently while Mattie listed every little thing she did, from eating French toast for breakfast, to brushing her teeth, to playing leap frog, to coloring in the pictures Sis drew for her.

"You want to see them?"

"I'd like nothing better, Princess."

Mattie came back at a dead run carrying a fistful of waded up paper which she handed to her dad one wrinkled picture at a time, and for each one, he made a huge fuss over it.

She poked the last one with her finger. "That's the bestest one of all."

"My, but you have become a real artist, Mattie."

"I am, aren't I?" she said, holding the colored scribbling up, tipping it right and left admiringly.

Leigh snickered. Uncle Bud gave her a stern look. Then he complimented Sis on her drawings, which made Sis blush, big time.

Then he looked at me. "Lainard, how would you like to come with me after lunch to feed the cattle?"

After blurting out, "You bet," I noticed Leigh grinning at me and realized my mistake. "I mean, yes, sir, I sure would."

66

He asked Sis if she wanted to go. She agreed, but didn't sound real keen on the idea.

When my cousins were out of school for the summer they helped Uncle Bud feed the cattle. So for them it was a chore, but I thought it sounded like great fun.

"Then we'd better get to it" he said. "Those cattle won't feed themselves."

Dana, who was lying in the grass out front waiting for us, went crazy when he saw us, barking and wiggling and generally getting underfoot. All of us, including Dana, climbed into the back of Uncle Bud's old rust bucket of a pickup truck. There's nothing like riding in the back of an open truck. Dana, with his nose up in the air taking in the smells, looked as pleased as punch.

The barn and feedlots were behind Uncle Bud's brother's place, the next house toward town from my cousins'. It was the sheriff's house, Tripp's uncle Pete, the guy I'd seen in the picture on the dining room wall. It only took us about two minutes to get to the barn because Uncle Bud drove so fast that when a bug hit my face it stung worse than a spitball.

At the barn we piled out of the truck and climbed onto the same hay wagon Tripp had taken us for a ride on. We climbed over a stack of hay bales so we could sit across the back of the wagon and let our legs dangle off the end.

Yelling to be heard over the noise of the old red Farmall tractor, Leigh warned Sis and me to hold on, and she wasn't kidding. We copied little Mattie who held on by slipping her hand under the twine of a hay bale.

I swear Uncle Bud pulled us across the field as fast as he'd driven the truck on the road, which made for a wild ride, as good as any at the county fair. When he stopped at the first pasture fence Mattie hopped off the wagon, even before it stopped. She unlatched and opened the fence then waited for Uncle Bud to pull the wagon through so she could close and re-latch it. Tripp grabbed her hand and yanked her up onto the wagon just before it lurched forward.

Our next stop was a waist-high metal water trough as long as the wagon. There was some yucky white stuff floating on it that looked much too gross even for cows to drink. I asked Tripp what it was.

"Cattle spit."

A herd of them grazing nearby looked up. Moments later they trotted toward us, a few of them at first, then dozens of them gathered around the wagon. Tripp was the first one to grab a hay bale, deftly breaking it open by using the twine it was tied with to pull the bale against his knee until it burst apart. By then Leigh had grabbed a bale and split it open. Not to be outdone, I tried one. It wasn't nearly as easy as they made it look. I pulled the bale against my knee. Next thing I knew I lost my grip and the bale fell off the wagon in one piece.

Uncle Bud, who'd been watching us from the tractor, told me to stay on the wagon. He got down, and elbowing his way through the cattle, broke the bale apart for them. I wanted to crawl in a hole, but Uncle Bud was pretty nice about it and so were my cousins. He didn't scold me for making a mess of it, and they didn't make fun of me for being a screw up. Of course, smarty-pants Sis had been smart enough to let Tripp and Leigh do the hard work. She helped Mattie kicked loose straw off the wagon.

CHURCH AND THE HOSPITAL

The next Sunday at breakfast Uncle Bud and Aunt Helen talked about the people they expected to see at church and the people they hoped to see at church. Neither Mattie, nor Tripp, nor Sis seemed upset about going to church, but Leigh and I were down at the mouth.

Being the first ones changed and out the front door, Tripp and I waited on the front porch for everyone else. The only differences between the way I looked that morning and the way I usually looked, was that my hair was combed, my cowlick was plastered down with Brylcream, my clothes were clean, and I had on dress shoes instead of sneakers.

Aunt Helen had Tripp wearing a tan sport coat with brown buttons, brown pants, and two-tone, brown and white shoes that looked like gangster shoes. Uncle Bud came out next, clean-shaven and wearing a white shirt and tan slacks, both of them freshly-ironed, with crisp neat seams. Uncle Bud had on a tie. Tripp and I wore clip on bowties.

The dress Aunt Helen was wearing that day may have been one of her around-the-house dresses, but her hair was extra curly and she had on earrings. After checking Tripp's hands, she gave him a hard time about the dirt under his fingernails. Lucky for him there wasn't enough time to clean them before we had to leave.

Sis came out wearing a dress with her hair all puffed up from drying it in giant curlers. Uncle Bud took one look at her and said, "I declare, Sarah, you are as pretty as a picture." I didn't see what all the fuss was about but it made her blush mightily.

Mattie and her mom came out next. Mattie's face and hands actually looked clean. Her wavy golden hair, tied in ponytails with little white ribbons, was free of knots and twigs. Her fluffy white dress had a bow in the back that was as half as big as her, and I didn't see a single grass stain on it or her bright white socks. Even her black shoes shone like they were brand-new, out-of-the-box.

Dana came to us out of the pasture in a frenzy of barking and drooling and tail wagging. Naturally Mattie was his first stop. But when she reached to pet him, Aunt Helen grabbed his collar and pulled him away. "Don't you dare pet him, Mattie. He's filthy."

Aunt Helen told Dana to sit, which he did, for about a second. When Uncle Bud told him to sit he stayed put.

Leigh, normally the first one of us to make it outside, was last. She came out wearing a blue dress with black shoes, and white socks like her little sister. Her light brown hair, hanging down almost to her waist, was brushed out smooth, and the sides were pulled back and clipped with a Barrette. She stood off by herself a little and avoided eye contact, like she'd been caught with her hand in the cookie jar.

About then Mom arrived. She came to get me and Sis because there wasn't enough room in the Ritcheys' car for all of us. Mother had on a long-sleeved light-pink dress with a matching jacket. It had little pink designs like clouds all over it. Her earrings were round and dangly and shiny, like two new nickels.

Pretty soon we were all on our way to church. The last time we'd been on that road with Mom I'd seen Margo at the Dawson's which got me thinking. "Hey. Mom?"

"Yes, dear?"

"Can I stay at the Dawson's for a few days?"

"Why would you want to do that? I thought you liked playing with your cousins."

I told her I missed Granddad, which was also true.

I should've known that Sis would figure it out and that she couldn't let it pass. "He wants to see Margo."

That got a startled-sounding "Oh," from Mom.

I told Sarah to shut up. That earned me a warning from Mom, but it didn't stop Sarah. "Buster's got a crush on her."

And that's why you should never tell your sister anything you don't want the world to know. I called my sister stupid. Mom told me to apologize, which wasn't fair. I said, "Sorry," to Sis then asked Mom, "So can I?'

"Can you what, dear?"

"Stay at the Dawson's for a few days?"

"We'll see."

That was as good as a no. We stopped on the way to church to get my mom's mom, Grandmother Thurman. As tall and skinny as my mom, Grandmother had on a long wispy-thin flowery dress with clunky-looking tie shoes. Her hair was pinned up in a swirl like Mom's and like Mom's there were no loose ends.

Instead of being all laughs and smiles like Grandma Dawson, Grandmother Thurman was always serious and always looked tired. Not that she was ever mean to Sis or me. She just didn't smile much. Mom said she never got to do fun stuff because Grandfather Thurman was sick just about all the time. So I didn't blame her for not smiling.

As if going to church hadn't already ruined my day, after church we went to see Grandfather Thurman in the hospital. All my memories of him were of a bony old man lying in a room as quiet as a closet and almost as dark, a place where making so much as a peep would land me in trouble.

Of course, Sis got to stay inside. She didn't make noise or bump into Grandmother's expensive things. Too bad for her, because it always smelled funny in their house, not smelly garbage funny, more like hot attic funny, probably from all the old stuff in there. Mostly it was boring old stuff, like paintings and little statues, the kind of stuff you see in museums. Mom said it was valuable stuff and that I'd be in big trouble if I broke any of it. And honestly, if I stayed inside I'd break something sooner or later, so Mom always took me inside just long enough to say hello then sent me outdoors.

Pretty soon we got to the hospital, which was made up of three buildings connected by covered walkways, each building as big as a department store. Even though Mother took the nearest parking space to the entrance that she could find, it was still a long walk, as far as going around the bases on a baseball diamond. And of course Mom and Grandmother kept us standing in the hot sun while they blabbed about the yellow rose bushes out front.

I couldn't tell from the inside of the hospital if we were in Florida or New York. I guess they're the same everywhere; big funny-smelling buildings with a million rooms and more than one elevator, and hallways going every which direction, not to mention all of the cool-looking machines. We took so many turns on the way to Grandfather's room I would've needed a map to find my way out.

Everything about the place bothered me; the way Grandfather looked, as gray and thin as a Halloween skeleton; Mother warning me to be quiet; having to stand because Mother and Grandmother got the only two chairs in the room; and of course, the nasty hospital smell.

On the drive down to Florida Mom told Sis and me that Grandmother Thurman took Grandfather to the hospital because he was too sick for her to take care of by herself. He had some disease like a sleeping sickness that he caught when they were on some island in the Pacific, that it kept coming back, and that every time it did it was worse.

After I'd been standing still forever, on the sorest feet ever, Aunt Helen showed up. But she came by herself so I still didn't have anyone to talk to.

A few minutes later a nurse came in. While she took

Grandfather's temperature she asked my Grandmother, "You were here until closing last night, weren't you?"

"Is that a problem?"

"Good heavens no. Let me know if you'll be staying late again tonight. I'll ask the night nurse to bring you a snack from the cafeteria with your husband's dinner."

Grandmother smiled at the nurse, what for most people would hardly have been considered a smile, but for Grandmother it was big. "I do plan to stay, thank you."

Before leaving the nurse said to Aunt Helen, "Thank the Lord y'all are devout Christians," in that sicky-sweet sounding way religious people sometimes have of talking.

Aunt Helen looked surprised at first, as though she'd been poked in an embarrassing spot. Then a frown appeared on her face. "Why do you say that?"

"The Good Lord will watch over him."

Sis was standing next to me. I whispered, "God must be really busy."

She kicked my foot and shook her head.

The nurse asked Aunt Helen, "Which of the Lord's houses do you attend?"

"A. M. E. Zion."

"I've been told that is a fine house of worship."

In the blink of an eye Aunt Helen's expression changed from suspicious to happy, even smiling at the nurse. "Oh, you simply must come hear one of Reverend Lee's sermons."

The nurse told Aunt Helen they'd been thinking of switching churches, because, "We have a new preacher whose sermons don't do God's message justice."

Aunt Helen would be happy all day because the nurse had agreed to try her church. You'd have thought she'd converted a pagan to Christianity. Don't ask me to explain it.

By then my poor feet ached so bad from standing that I leaned on Grandfather's bedside table for relief. And wouldn't you know it, the dang thing had wheels. So even though I barely touched it, it got away from me, rolling across the room to crash

73

into Grandfather's bed. Mother led me out of the room, scolding me as she dragged me down the hall by my ear to a waiting room, where she told me to stay until she came for me.

The people in the room stared at me, and who could blame them? I wanted to crawl into a hole, but there was nowhere to hide. There were six other people in the room: a kindergarten-aged boy and his mother, two old women sitting together, one of them knitting, and a young man standing by the windows holding a toddler, pointing at something outside.

Fortunately, the waiting room smelled better than Grandfather's room and there were even some old copies of Boy's Life on the table next to me. Someone had already done all the puzzles, but the jokes were funny, and I had always liked doing the games where you find the differences between two pictures. But best of all, I could sit down. That alone made it worth the embarrassment. But by the time I had finished the second magazine I needed to pee.

THE MEAN KID

I checked the hallway - no bathroom in sight in either direction, but Grandfather's room was to the left. I walked to the right so Mom wouldn't see me walk past his door. I eventually found a bathroom down one of the side hallways.

As big as a school bathroom, it had four urinals, four stalls, and six sinks, and best of all it was empty. Of course as soon as I started to pee a big kid came in. He had to be several years older than me; because, besides being half a head taller, he had real peach fuzz on his chin. With his hair greased into a pompadour like Jimmy Dean, and his tight tee shirt showing off his bulging arm muscles, he looked like a troublemaker. I pretended he wasn't there and hoped he'd do the same with me.

He didn't. "You got someone here who's dying?"

I suppose he was trying to be friendly, but if I said anything he'd know I was a Yankee. So I shook my head and went to the sink to wash my hands and hoped that would be the end of it. It wasn't.

"Not very friendly, are ya?"

I looked at him. He was glaring at me. I looked away and said, "Sorry."

Out of the corner of my eye I saw that he'd stopped on his way to the sink and was staring at me. "You're a Yankee, aren't ya?"

As I hurried for the door, wiping my hands dry on my pants on the way, he said, "Hey kid."

I stopped at the door to look back. He was waving an open

jackknife at me. I left in a hurry. As the door closed behind me I heard him laughing and wished I was big enough to teach him a lesson.

I hesitated at the door to the waiting room, because if I sat in my old seat the mean kid would see me if he walked past. Except for a scruffy-looking guy with shaggy hair sitting near the old ladies, the same people were there as before. I sat near the old ladies where I couldn't be seen by someone in hallway. I felt safer having other people around.

Because I'd left an empty seat between me and the old women, I ended up sitting facing the scruffy guy. He had big rough hands, a tattoo of a striking cobra on his neck, and like the kid in the bathroom, he had dark, mean looking eyes.

Dressed in working men's clothes, like Grandpa Dawson wore, he looked about the same age as my dad, but unlike my dad, he had a beard. It had odd-looking orangey-red streaks in it under his mouth. I once met a relative at Grandpa Dawsons' who had a beard streaked like that. Grandpa told me the streaks were from chewing tobacco dribbling in his beard when he spit.

Scruffy stared right at me. I pretended to look at a picture of a sailboat on the wall over his head, figuring he'd look away soon. When I checked he was still staring at me. I looked at my feet and tried real hard not to look at him again, which made not looking even harder.

After a while the nurse who'd been talking to Aunt Helen came in and sat next to Scruffy, close enough for me to hear her say. "They go to that A. M. E. Zion church I told you about. I want us to go there this Sunday."

He yanked on her arm, pulling her ear close to his mouth, whispering at her angrily. "I don't give a good crap which church they go to. You were supposed to find out if the old bag's staying late tonight."

The nurse squirmed and tried to pull her arm away. "You're hurting me."

"Not half as much as I'm gonna hurt you if you don't do like I told you."

"I did. I asked her. She's staying until closing tonight."

When Scruffy let go of her arm she rubbed the spot. He told her to get back to work, that they shouldn't been seen together. I pretended to tie my shoe so she wouldn't see my face. She was still rubbing her arm when she left the room.

A few minutes later I smelled Blackjack gum, my favorite gum in the whole world. It was the kindergarten kid. My stomach grumbled at the smell of it. It had been a million years since breakfast and I was starving. I decided to chance it and go ask Mom for a nickel so I could get some Blackjack from the vending machine by the front entrance.

I had just been thinking how lucky I was I hadn't seen the mean kid again. But when I stepped into the hallway, as sure as night follows day, there he was talking to Sis. I ducked back into the waiting room and peeked around the door to watch them. They sure acted weird; Sis smiling at him, happy as a kid opening presents, and the mean kid grinning as he looked her over.

All of a sudden he looked my direction. I ducked into the waiting room and hurried back to my seat then watched nervously for him out of the corner of my eye, hoping he wouldn't come in. But sure as every schoolyard has bully, he did, walking right toward me. I looked away and held my breath.

He kicked the leg of my chair when he walked past me. It might've looked like an accident to someone watching, but I knew he did it on purpose. Anyway, it took me by surprise and got me to look at him. He had his back to Sis so she didn't know he whispered something to me, "Stinking Yankee coward. Lucky for you there's people around." The he sat next to Scruffy. That figured.

Sis was standing at the door. She had always been the quiet, serious type, so the big, goofy smile on her face looked really out of place. She called me over with a wave of her hand. I couldn't wait to get out of there. On the way to Grandfather's room, I told her that the kid she'd been talking to had been mean to me.

That got a distracted, "Huh?" from her, as though she'd

had trouble hearing me.

"He was mean to me."

"Who was? What are you talking about?"

"The kid you were talking to in the hallway."

"You're being silly."

"Am not," I said.

"I bet you don't like him because of his Southern accent. Remember what I told Mattie about people who seem different."

"Your boyfriend's a creep with a Southern accent. Good for you"

She spun around, and changing from her usual decent self into a real snot in less than an instant, like that Jekyll and Hyde guy, she called me a liar like then stormed off.

I hustled to catch up with her. There wasn't much point in telling her about the knife. She wouldn't have believed me anyway. So I told her I heard Scruffy and the nurse talking about Grandmother. She told me to hurry up.

I couldn't possibly keep up with those Giraffe legs of hers, so I half yelled, "Scruffy asked that nurse lady if Grandmother was going to stay late."

Sis stopped and turned around. She gave me one of Mother's, "you are in big trouble," looks.

"Well, don't you think that's strange?"

She said, "Button it. Mom's waiting for us" then walked away.

I didn't even try to keep up with her.

A ROBBERY

Mother sent me home from the hospital with Aunt Helen. Sis stayed at the hospital with Mom, which meant she'd be spending the night with Mom at Grandmother Thurman's. But first, poor Sis would have to stay late at the hospital. Mom said they'd eat in the cafeteria downstairs. If it was as good as a Morrison's that would've almost made it worth staying.

No, I take that back, because if I stayed with them I'd have to sleep at Grandmother Thurman's, and it would be really scary sleeping with breakable expensive stuff all around me. Lucky for me Mom didn't want me at Grandmother's house, and lucky for me Aunt Helen had to get back to fix dinner for Uncle Bud. It meant I didn't have to stay at the hospital any longer.

As we got out of the car at my cousin's house, Aunt Helen told me to warn my cousins not to go anywhere because we'd be eating soon. I found them in the playroom arguing, well Leigh and Mattie were arguing. They'd been playing a kid's card game called war. Mattie had accused Leigh of cheating, which I didn't think was even possible playing that game.

I told Leigh about Sis acting weird at the hospital.

"What do you mean, weird?"

"Well at first when I tried to talk to her she acted groggy, like some alien had taken over her mind. Then, all of a sudden, she got mad, and for no reason."

"What was she doing before that?"

"Talking to some kid."

"What about?"

"I don't know, I couldn't hear them. But that's when she was acting weird."

"Weird, how?"

"Like a red-faced, giggling little girl."

Leigh grinned, said, "She has a crush on him."

"My sister?"

"Don't tell me. Let me guess. She fussed with her hair or her clothes?"

"Yeah, how did you know?"

"The fussing made her feel girlish."

"Huh?"

"It's called flirting, silly."

"How come she got mad when I said she liked him?"

"Because it's true and she was embarrassed about it, which proves it."

I didn't want to think about my sister and some guy that way. And didn't it figure that the first kid my sister ever liked would be a real creep.

From then until dinner we played Go Fish, a game we could all play with Mattie. After a dinner of chicken and rice and Jell-O we chased fireflies until it was too dark to see where we were going, and the air had turned a little too cool. Not that I needed a jacket, but it felt too cool for a summer night, which not only meant the day was ending, but that the summer was too.

The phone rang during breakfast the next morning, I knew it was something serious when Aunt Helen said "Oh dear Lord."

Leigh asked her Mom who it was.

Aunt Helen told Leigh, "Hush up" then said into the phone, "Do you want Bud to come over there?" then after a pause, "Well okay, if you're sure, but I'll have him tell Pete about it."

After she hung up the phone she stood there staring at it. Leigh asked her what was wrong.

"That was Lizbeth. Someone broke into mother's house.

Everyone's okay. It happened while they were at the hospital."

When we finished breakfast Aunt Helen told us kids to go play in the playroom and that she was going to find Uncle Bud.

When we got to the playroom Leigh tossed a deck of cards on their folding table. "Even Mattie can play slapjack."

Leigh offered to deal the cards, which surprised me because that put her at a disadvantage. As for Mattie, I didn't think she stood a chance against us older kids. Boy was I wrong. Her little hand shot out like a snake's head when Leigh put down the jack of spades. I concentrated extra hard but Mattie got the jack of hearts too. Tripp snagged the third jack. Leigh got the last one.

We played that game half a dozen times before Aunt Helen called us for dinner. I slapped a few jacks but never won a game. Mattie won twice. After dinner we played Croquet. By the time Aunt Helen called us in for bed it was getting too dark to see the hoops.

Next morning, everyone had French toast for breakfast, even Uncle Bud. While Tripp drowned a slice of French toast with syrup, Leigh asked her parents if there was any news on the break-in.

Aunt Helen's comment, "Thank the lord no one got hurt," got me wondering why people always thanked the Lord when things went well, but never blamed him when things went bad. It would be like my parents praising me when I did something well and blaming Sis when I did something bad. Nice to dream about; but never gonna happen.

We got the latest on the break-in from Uncle Bud. "Pete came to see me this morning while I was feeding calves. He said he caught the kid who did it."

Aunt Helen's coffee cup stopped halfway to her lips. "That was fast."

"Well, he did have some help. One of the neighbor's boys told his dad he saw an older kid from school sneaking around Mrs. Thurman's house, and that the kid was a known troublemaker. The boy's dad called Pete."

"Dear me," Aunt Helen said. "High school kids robbing old ladies. What's the world coming to?"

Mattie grabbed a slice of French toast with her fingers. It earned her a frown from Aunt Helen which she ignored because she was busy, carefully pouring syrup on it in a swirl pattern.

Aunt Helen asked Uncle Bud, "What about the boy? What'll happen to him?"

"I don't know. Pete didn't say."

"People sure can be dumb," she said, saying the word "dumb" with emphasis and stretching it out with an exaggerated drawl.

Later that morning Tripp and I decided to make bows and arrows. We were checking the bushes along their backyard fence for springy branches when Sis called my name. Standing near the carport she waved at me to follow her then disappeared around the corner of the house. I found her sitting on the Ritcheys' front steps.

Afraid Mom was coming to take us somewhere uncomfortable, I hesitated to ask her what she wanted.

She handed me a greeting card, said, "That's for Margo."

First I thanked her then I asked her where she got it. I wanted to be sure she hadn't said anything to Mom about me and Margo.

"When we were at the hospital visiting Grandfather Thurman, Mom sent me to the waiting room to get you. I snuck down to the gift shop first."

I wondered why she was being nice to me after I'd been mean to her about her boyfriend, even if I had good reason to be. On the outside of the card it read, "I was thinking of you today. I thought you'd want to know."

I opened it up. "Hey, it's blank inside."

"That's so you can write your own note. She'll appreciate it more if it's your own thoughts."

My mind went blank immediately, as blank as the inside of the card. "What do you think I should write?"

"What'd I just say?"

"But I can't think of anything."

Sis rolled her eyes and shook her head. "If she was here right now, what would you say to her?"

"I'd go brain-dead."

She stood up, said, "Then I can't help you," as though she was about to leave.

"Hey, what did that guy say to you?"

"What guy?"

"The kid you were talking to in the hallway. You know, outside the waiting room at the hospital."

Even though she said, "None of your business," I knew it must've been something good because her face turned bright red.

"I'll never be able to think of anything good, not without some help."

Sis rolled her eyes and went inside. I felt a little bit bad for picking on her when she'd been nice enough to get me the card. Sis was just about the smartest person I knew, and if she thought that's what I had to do to impress Margo, then by golly that's what I was going to do. Of course I had once thought I could play a part in a school play, but the first time I walked out on the stage and looked at the audience, I got so scared I not only forgot my lines I almost fainted.

I liked Margo, but telling her so, even in a card, was scarier than being on stage or taking a leaky boat out on a swamp full of gators. Besides, the chance I'd think of something clever to write was somewhere between none at all and a lot less than that.

After staring at the card for a while I did figure out two important things: the more you like a girl the harder it is to tell her so, and that I'd regret it if I didn't tell her. And for that I needed a pencil. I remembered seeing an old schoolroom desk in my cousin's playroom that I could write on. Of course, on the way there I imagined Margo reading my note and being mightily impressed.

The desk turned out to be much smaller than I remembered, so small I could barely squeeze my legs in under it. Inside the desk I found a pencil mixed in with the crumpled papers and broken crayons . I opened the card with the wildly unrealistic expectations of a kid on Christmas Eve.

At the top I wrote in my very best handwriting, "Hi Margo." Leaving some empty space below that I wrote, "I like you. You're very pretty." Writing that I felt almost as giddy as I had when she touched my hand, even if it had been an accident. Feeling mighty proud of what I'd written, I printed my name at the bottom of the card with real satisfaction.

I was so sure she'd like it that I read it out loud. I got as far as, "I like you," before I felt my face get red hot. Reading, "You're pretty," out loud was too much. I had to get out of there, and fast, before anyone saw me and asked what I was doing.

As I wriggled myself out of the desk I tore my pants on something. Of course, Mom would be furious. I'd have to make up an excuse to explain it. On the way out of the room I threw the card in the garbage and vowed to forget Margo, and never, ever like another girl.

ALLIGATOR HUNTERS FIND A BODY

Breakfast the next morning was interrupted by someone knocking on the front door. Aunt Helen and Sis stayed at the table. The rest of us followed Uncle Bud, crowding around him when he answered the door. Two men were standing on the porch. I saw an airboat on a trailer in the driveway, something I'd only ever seen in magazines. The men offered to pay Uncle Bud to use his access road to the lake.

Aunt Helen called us back to the table. She said our eggs were getting cold and, "Y'all had better come eat them now because I'm done cooking."

Back at the table I asked Tripp about the airboat.

"They use them to hunt gators."

"Man, what I wouldn't give for a ride in their boat."

"Speaking of gators," Aunt Helen said, "When we get a couple of days of rain the pastures flood. Then the gators come out of the swamp. After one especially hard rain I found one under our car, right out there in our carport."

I wished for rain, and lots of it, even prayed for it, because you never know, there might be something to the whole God and praying thing. Sis asked Aunt Helen what she did about the alligator.

"I wouldn't have even known about it if it hadn't been for Dana barking up a storm. I assumed it was a raccoon or a possum. Raccoons get into our garbage. And damned if they aren't the smartest animals. Doesn't matter how we tie the lids on, they can still get them open. And what a mess. We get an occasional possum too. Aren't they just the cutest things you ever saw? But dumb? I swear I don't know what God was thinking when he made them."

Leigh said, "Momma?" with a hint of a snicker.

"Oh my, I seem to have gotten side-tracked again. Well to make a long story short, I took the broom out to chase the raccoon away. I couldn't see it from this side of the car so I walked around to the other side, and Lord almighty, I damn near stepped on that gator. I hate to think what would've happened if we'd been going someplace that day and the kids had gone out to the car ahead of me."

I asked her what happened after that.

You can usually count on Aunt Helen for an exciting story, but not that time. "I called the game warden. Three men came and got him."

I asked her if they killed it.

"No, but it took them the better part of an hour to get it out from under the car and tied up well enough so they could get it into their truck."

Aunt Helen sent us outside after breakfast. Mattie talked us into playing hide-and-seek. I'd already tired of that when Dana's barking alerted us to someone else coming. We raced around the house to the front porch, getting there in time to see the gator hunter's truck kicking up dust as they drove in from the road, fast, and without their airboat.

The two men didn't get out of their truck. Instead, the guy on our side rolled his window down. I guess they assumed we were all Ritchey kids because he told us to go get our dad.

Mattie ran inside to get Uncle Bud. When he came out, we crowded around him to hear what the men had to say.

"We found a dead body."

"One of my steers?"

"No sir," the man said, looking around at us kids before

answering, as though he was unsure about something. "It's definitely a person."

Uncle Bud told us kids to go in the house.

Tripp ran for the door. Leigh and Mattie ran after him. Sis and I followed, but walked.

After Tripp breathlessly told his mom that the hunters found a dead person, she asked him, "Y'all are sure that's what they said?"

We bombarded her with a chorus of, "Yes, ma'am's," as Uncle Bud came into the room. Aunt Helen told us to go outdoors.

"But Mom," Tripp said, "we just came in."

Before she'd finished saying, "Then you have to sit quiet," Leigh and Tripp raced for the best seat in the room, a bentwood rocking chair. Leigh got there first and stuck her tongue out at Tripp.

Aunt Helen told them to behave then asked Uncle Bud, "Is it true that those men found a dead person?"

He nodded his head. "They're going to wait out front until Pete gets here so they can go with him to show him where they found it."

He dialed the phone then after a pause said, "Sheriff Ritchey, please."

Then he said, "This is his brother, Bud" then, "Oh, I see. Well, you'd better send someone out here. Some gator hunters found a body on our property."

After he hung up he told Aunt Helen, "Deputy Mayville's coming."

"Why would Pete send a deputy?"

"Pete didn't show up for work this morning."

Aunt Helen grimaced and shook her head. "Sure is a lot of odd things happening lately."

She looked around the table at us kids. "Like you kids falling asleep at breakfast Friday morning. Y'all got something you want to tell us?"

I kept my eyes glued to a crumb on the table in front of me,

87

hoping she wouldn't ask me any questions.

She singled Tripp out. "I know y'all were up late Thursday night. I want to know what you were doing."

He shrugged his shoulders.

When Aunt Helen threatened to get the ruler he opened up like a sinkhole. "We saw two men stealing water."

Leigh told him, "Hush up," but the cat was already out of the bag.

Aunt Helen told Leigh to keep quiet and Tripp that it was his last chance before she got the ruler. "You kids were at the lake Friday night, weren't you?"

Tripp looked down at this plate. "Yes, ma'am."

"What on God's green earth were you thinking?"

Uncle Bud asked Tripp how he knew the men were stealing water.

"They had a big hose running down to the lake from one of those firetrucks that pump water. Another hose ran into the woods."

The way Aunt Helen looked at us, kind of sideways, I know she suspected us of hiding something. Parents have ways of finding things out, like surprising you with a question when you're not expecting it. But that shoe would drop some other time. Aunt Helen told us kids to go outdoors, that she needed to talk to Uncle Bud.

Tripp was the first one up, rushing for the door saying, "Last one out is a rotten egg."

Mattie yelled, "No fair."

Leigh yelled, "Cheater."

BAD NEWS FOR UNCLE BUD

When we'd gathered out near the bridge Sis asked no one in particular, "I wonder who it is."

After hearing Leigh's suggestion, that a Momma gator caught some guy taking eggs from her nest, I pictured a man on his hands and knees near the swamp and his back to the water. A ripple in the water came toward him, moving faster and getting bigger until an alligator as long as a car exploded out of the lake behind him in a giant spray of water, its mouth open wide enough to swallow him whole.

Sis said kinda smart-alecky like, "I bet someone took your boat out and it sank, and when he tried to swim for it the gators got him."

When Tripp suggested, "Could be somebody who got bit by a rattlesnake," Leigh poo pooed it, saying, "Nah, he would've had time to get help."

Mattie pushed her way into the middle to state with absolute certainty, that, "It was a goblin." which earned her a snicker from Leigh. Mattie retaliated by sticking her tongue out.

A few minutes later Leigh suggested we play tag. Mattie's little hand shot up like a rocket. "Ooh, ooh, I wanna be it."

Leigh let Mattie have her way because she threatened to scream. Mattie chased Sis, who let herself be tagged. Then Sis chased Leigh, the two of them easily leaping over the ditch. When Mattie tried to jump it she landed waist deep in the weeds with a loud squish.

Tripp wrapped an arm around Mattie and tugged, pulling her right out of her boots. He asked me to get her boots while he held her off the ground. I knelt down and tried to put her boots on but she was having too much fun wiggling her feet and giggling. Tripp dropped her on her butt in the grass. I tossed her boots at her feet.

After yelling, "poopy-pants," at us Mattie put her boots on.

By then Leigh and Sis were doing a dance, Leigh backing up and sidestepping as Sis tried to tag her, managing to stay just out of Sis' reach. The two of them laughing like fools. I hadn't seen Sis having that much fun playing a kid's game in years.

Mattie ran over to join them, doing some exaggerated sidestepping of her own. Sis made a show of trying to tag Mattie. It was like watching a slow motion cartoon, Sis's hand reaching for Mattie and Mattie dodging it, and that happening over and over, while Mattie laughed hysterically.

Tripp got too close to Sis and got tagged. He chased Leigh until we heard Dana barking. We ran out front to see who was coming. A sheriff's cruiser was speeding toward the house, kicking up a big cloud of dust. We stood on the front porch to watch, turning away when the dust cloud blew past us.

A young guy in a tan uniform with official-looking patches on his shoulders and a hat with a wide flat brim got out of the car. He flashed a faint smile at us and nodded his head as he walked past.

Mattie, who barely came up to the man's waist, followed him to the door, asked him, "Are you a sheriff like my Uncle Pete?"

He rang the doorbell then took his hat off and smiled at her. "No, ma'am, I'm a deputy. I work for your uncle."

Uncle Bud came out and shook hands with the deputy, who said, "Quintin Mayville, sir."

The two of them walked over to the gator hunter's truck.

The four men talked for a few minutes then Quintin got back in his cruiser and followed the truck out to the road. They turned left and disappeared.

Mattie poked Leigh on the shoulder and yelled "You're it" then ran for the back yard with us in pursuit, except for Sis who walked.

When Dana announced the arrival of another car about an hour later, we ran back around to the front to see who it was. It turned out to be Quintin coming back. He asked my cousins to get their dad. When Uncle Bud came out Quintin led him over to his car so we couldn't hear them talking. Quintin said something to Bud then the two men stood there, Uncle Bud with his back to us looking at the sky near the tree line and Quintin studying his feet.

We sat on the front steps to wait. Mattie sat on the bottom one. Sis sat next to her but on the top step, so her feet were next to Mattie's. Leigh and Tripp and I sat on the middle step. Pretty soon Aunt Helen came outside and walked over to join Uncle Bud and Quintin. She said something to Uncle Bud. Quintin said something to her then got in his car and drove away. She stood next to Uncle Bud with her arm around his waist. Neither of them moved a muscle or said a thing for the longest time.

After a while she gave him a squeeze then came over to us kids and asked, "Did any of you see anyone besides the two men stealing water the night you went to the lake?"

It got her a few mumbled, "No, ma'ams."

"How about you, Tripp?"

"What?"

"Did you see anyone else?"

She knew he was hiding something. She had to after he looked at Leigh and grimaced.

"Either you tell me or I get the ruler."

That did it. And who could blame him? "There's a squatter living in Great Granddaddy's cabin." `

"Why in heaven's name didn't you kids tell us that before?"

Leigh and Tripp both shrugged their shoulders. Aunt

Helen sighed and shook her head. She told us to stay where we were then went to talk to Uncle Bud. Mattie swatted Leigh's leg.

"Hey, what's that for?"

"It's your fault if Amu gets in trouble."

"Tripp's the one who ratted on him."

"If you didn't make us go to Great Granddaddy's cabin we never would've found him. Then Tripp couldn't have ratted on him. That makes it your fault."

Surprisingly, Leigh didn't put up a fight. Instead, she leaned over, rested her elbows on her knees and looked down at her feet.

Uncle Bud headed for the house. He had a funny look on his face, not funny "ha, ha," more of a lost look. We scooched over so he could get past us. Aunt Helen stood in front of us. She told my cousins to go inside and wait for her in the dining room; that she'd be in in a few minutes. They grumbled about it but went. That left Sis and me with Aunt Helen, who said to us, "I'm going to have Lizbeth come get you."

Sis asked her what was wrong.

"The body they found was Bud's brother Pete."

I had no idea what to say to Aunt Helen, But Sis being an almost grownup did. "Oh, Aunt Helen, I am so sorry."

I said, "Me too."

Sis asked how he died.

"We don't know yet. But Bud and the kids will be very upset. You can help by waiting out here for Lizbeth. She'll be taking you to Momma's or the Dawsons' for the day."

After a hot, thirsty forever, Deputy Mayville came back. Aunt Helen and Uncle Bud came back outside. They'd have heard Dana barking. Quintin parked about ten feet from where Sis and I were sitting on the steps. Amu was in the back seat of his car. I wondered if Quinten told him it was us kids who'd ratted him out.

Aunt Helen and Uncle Bud walked over to the driver's door as Quintin was getting out. I walked over and stood next to the back passenger side door. Up close in the daylight Amu didn't

92

look so scary, just a shabby-looking, skinny guy whose clothes looked as though he'd slept in them. The lines in his face looked deeper and his hair looked grayer, and his hands were behind his back. I caught a glimpse of the handcuffs. Mostly he looked frightened.

Uncle Bud pointed at Amu, asked Quintin, "What's he doing here?"

"I found him hiding in a cabin about half a mile from where they found Sheriff Ritchey."

"You think he killed Pete?"

"I think maybe your brother confronted him and they got into a fight."

"How would Pete have known about him?"

"Maybe your brother saw his fire from the Williston Cutoff.

"What fire?"

"Someone's been burning wood in a fire pit outside the cabin."

"It's been years since anyone lived in Granddad's old place."

"The ash in the pit was still powdery, so there was a fire there since the last rain. Otherwise it would've caked up."

"Even so, I doubt Pete could've seen it from the Cutoff."

I asked Sis what the Williston Cutoff was.

"I don't know. We'll ask Leigh some time."

Quintin told Uncle Bud, "That fellow put up a fight when I tried to question him. Why would he do that if he's not guilty?"

"He's a squatter. He's afraid of going to jail for vagrancy."

"Just the same, that cabin is near enough to the lakeshore where your brother's body was found."

"That doesn't mean he did it."

Quintin pointed back over his shoulder at Amu with his thumb. "How do you explain the bruise on his cheek and that scar on his lip?"

Aunt Helen walked over to the backseat window where I was standing and leaned down close to the window. "Deputy

Mayville's right, Bud. It looks like he's been in a fight."

"Pete's a big man, Quintin." Uncle Bud choked up a little then corrected himself. "Was a big man."

"I know, sir."

"My point is; that fella in the back of your car's a lightweight. I don't see how he could've gotten the upper hand on my brother."

"Guy's a squatter and a vagrant. I'm taking him in on that. And I'll bet you dollars to doughnuts that the DA will charge him for killing Pete."

Aunt Helen asked Quintin to check on the two guys us kids saw at the lake, then told him, "If Pete found them stealing water he would've tried to arrest them."

After taking out a small pad of paper and a pen Quintin asked Uncle Bud if he knew who the men were.

"They would've have been working for the Branfords who have a place on the Williston Cutoff that borders our place. We caught them stealing water the last time we had a drought, about two years ago.

With a nod toward his car, Quintin said, "After I take this guy back to town, I'll see what I can find out" then left.

Uncle Bud and Aunt Helen went inside. Sis and I waited on the steps for Mom, neither of us doing or saying much, except for my stomach, which was growling so loud I thought sure Sis could hear it. It had been hours since I'd had French toast. But I couldn't very well complain about being hungry after what had happened.

A REALLY MEAN TRICK

A few minutes later Dana announced the approach of another car. This time it was Mom coming to get Sis and me. On the way into town I opened the backseat window and put my hand out, tipping it so the wind caught it and pushed it up and down like a kite. Mom told me to keep my hand in the car. I asked her why we were going to the Dawsons'.

"We're only staying for a minute. I've got something for Mrs. Dawson then we're going to Mother's," by which she meant Grandmother Thurman's.

"Aw, Mom, why do we have to go there?"

"To get you out of Aunt Helen's hair."

I thought about getting in Aunt Helen's hair for real. It was another one of those things grownups said that made no sense.

With any luck, we'd be the only people at the Dawsons', and if Mom let me stay there and took Sis to Grandmother Thurman's with her, it would just be me with Grandpa. I told Mom, "I hope no one else is there."

Sis called me a weirdo.

I stuck my tongue out at her. "So are you, and double too."

Mom looked at us in the rearview mirror. "That's enough, both of you."

Driving through Gainesville I shaded my eyes with my hand because the sunlight reflected off of the downtown store windows was blinding. Once when Mom stopped for a traffic light I saw heat shimmering off the pavement and put my hand out of the car window. I could feel the heat rising off the pavement. It would be too hot to do anything at the Ritcheys' except run through the sprinkler.

When we turned onto Grandpa's street, I saw two people sitting in his rockers. My stomach flip-flopped when I recognized Margo. For one exciting, scary moment I thought about telling her that I liked her. Then I spotted Tommy Lee in the other rocker and hope turned to dread.

As we got out of the car Mother told us we weren't staying long. I pretended I'd left something in the car and went back to look for it because I wanted Mom and Sis to be inside when I said "Hi" to Margo - I didn't want them to hear the very clever thing I knew I'd think of to say to her.

I got out of the car when I saw Mom and Sis go inside even though I still hadn't thought of anything clever to say. I wished I'd known Margo would be at Grandpa's, wished I'd been daydreaming about Margo on the way to Grandpa's instead of spaceships and little green men, wished I wasn't such a screw up.

With Margo and Tommy Lee watching me, the walk across the yard to the porch made me so nervous that by the time I got to the porch steps I couldn't remember crossing the yard. And dumb me, I looked at Margo a moment too long, tripping on the bottom step right in front of her, breaking my fall with my hands. The way Tommy Lee laughed about it, you'd have thought it was a Three Stooges move.

Margo didn't laugh. She just said, "Hi, Leonard" then smiled at me.

The way my face was burning, I bet it looked bright red, as red as my mom's reddest lipstick. I said, "Hi, Margo" without looking at her.

Grinning at me, Tommy Lee said, "Well if it isn't the little Yankee boy." Somehow he knew I liked Margo. I don't know how he figured it out, but he had, same as Sis. I didn't like the thought of him being as smart as Sis, not one bit. I sat on the top step, but if there had been a big enough rock there, I would've crawled under that instead.

Then Tommy Lee asked me if I'd ever been hunting. I shook my head.

"Well I've been lots of times; even have my own gun."

I said, "So," pretending I wasn't impressed. I was, of course, and I was sure Margo was too.

"Got me a whole passel of squirrels," he said. "Even bagged a wild pig."

I loved Margo's reaction, that she couldn't possibly like someone who would hurt a poor innocent animal. It sounded like something my sister would say. The way Tommy Lee glared at me you'd have thought it was my fault he'd made a fool of himself. It got quiet again after that, until looking at something behind me, Margo made kissing sounds. I turned around to see why. A scrawny-looking black and white cat walking through the yard had stopped to look at us, hoping for a handout probably.

All of a sudden, it jumped two feet off the ground, yowling as it spun sideways in midair, as though something had hurt the poor thing, except that there wasn't any grass under the live oak tree, so nothing could have snuck up on it. I might have thought the cat was rabid if I hadn't heard the telltale slapping sound a slingshot makes when the rubber strap hits your wrist.

Thinking that I'd look like a hero if I got the cat for Margo, I jumped down off the porch. It shied away. I held my hand out to it. It didn't come to me until I made the same stupid kissing sounds Margo had made. When it rubbed against my leg, I picked it up. Instead of petting it I should have been watching Tommy Lee, because he got in a lucky shot, hitting the cat with another BB while I was holding it, and just as Mom and Sarah came outside.

The cat yowled then went wild, all four legs flailing with its claws out, scratching the hell out of my arms. It pushed off to get away, scratching my stomach right through my shirt. And Mom and Sis had seen the whole thing.

Then things really went to crap. The cat ran off. I started to yell at Tommy Lee, but only got as far as, "Hey," before Mom yelled at me. "Leonard, you leave that cat alone."

I tried to object but Mom told me, "You get in the car, right now, Buster. And I don't want to hear another peep out of you."

If Mom scolding me in front of Margo wasn't bad enough, Tommy Lee grinned at me. It must have been great fun for him. Pretending that he was standing in front of me, I kicked at the dirt. Dry sandy soil flew up in a spray that sounded like sleet when it hit the car parked in front of ours. Of course, I'd catch hell for that too. If Mom hadn't been behind me I would've seen her reaching for my ear and ducked. I thought she was going to pull it clean off my head the way she yanked on it.

Things couldn't possibly get any worse, so of course they did. While I scrambled to keep up so Mom wouldn't do any permanent damage to my ear, she asked me if I wanted a spanking, loud enough for Margo to hear. And if that wasn't bad enough, she said, "And don't think I won't do it, right here in front of your friends."

As I was getting into the car I noticed that Tommy Lee was grinning like the cat who swallowed the canary. I bet his mom wouldn't dare embarrass him like that. With my face on fire from the shame, I slumped down in the seat to hide. Luckily for me Sarah was sitting on the side of the back seat nearest the porch so it would be harder for Margo to see me. I looked back for one last glimpse of Margo as Mother turned the corner onto Main Street.

Glancing at me in the mirror Mother asked, "Whatever possessed you to hurt that poor cat?"

"I didn't."

"I saw you."

"It scratched me."

"It wouldn't do that without a reason."

I was so upset by then that my voice cracked when I blurted out, "Ask Tommy Lee."

"What's he got to do with the price of tea in China?"

I wanted to scream, "That's a stupid thing to say," or better yet, hit something, but then I'd just get in even more trouble.

I felt a lump in my throat. My lip quivered. Until I was sure I wouldn't cry, all I dared say was, "A slingshot, that's what,"

"You'd better start making sense, Buster."

"I was going to bring the cat to Margo so she could pet it. It scratched me because Tommy Lee hit it with a pellet from his slingshot."

"His slingshot?"

"Yeah."

"Oh dear."

"So you embarrassed me for nothing."

"Oh, Leonard," she said, all gooey-sounding, "I am so sorry I said those things in front of your friends."

"They're not my friends, not anymore."

I looked out the car window and tried really hard to forget the absolute worst day of my life.

Mom looked at me in the rearview mirror, asked me if I'd heard her apologize.

"Yeah, okay," but it wasn't okay. Nothing she could say would ever make up for embarrassing me in front of Margo worse than I'd ever been embarrassed in front of anyone, ever. I was super duper glad I hadn't sent Margo the card Sis gave me.

And of course, Mom just wouldn't drop it. "That's quite the pout, Buster. If you're not careful you'll trip on that lip."

I wanted to scream.

BAIL FOR AMU

Later, after we'd taken Grandmother Thurman to a Morrison cafeteria, which is a good place to eat because you can skip all the yucky-looking food and load your plate with stuff you like, Mom took us back out to my cousins' house. On the way, right in the middle of downtown Gainesville, Mom starting singing that old church song, Amazing Grace. She sang so loudly with her window open that people we passed on the street stopped to watch us go by. Of course, Mom being the opposite of Sis, didn't seem to care. I slouched down in the seat to hide.

While mother was distracted with her own singing Sis went, "Psssst."

I gave her a dirty look. Whispering to me, she askedwhy I threw Margo's card away.

"How'd you know I threw it out?"

"I saw it in the garbage."

I looked out my window and hoped she'd leave me alone.

She didn't. "Do you want me to send it to Margo?"

"You took it out of the garbage?"

"I think you should send it to her, especially now."

I couldn't send it to her, especially now. I shook my head doubly hard to be sure she got the message. It was late afternoon by the time we got back to the Ritcheys'. Leigh and Tripp were sitting on the back steps looking as hang-dogged as I'd ever seen anybody look.

Sis said to them, "I'm sorry about your uncle."

Leigh looked at us a little bit teary-eyed. "Deputy Mayville

100

thinks Amu did it."

Sis asked her, "Did you tell your dad that Amu rescued Mattie from those guys at the lake?"

Tripp shook his head, muttered, "We cain't" then said, "We're already in big trouble for sneaking out. But we'll really catch hell if Dad finds out that we took the boat out, and that those guys chased us and grabbed Mattie."

Sarah insisted that we tell Uncle Bud what happened, but Leigh wasn't having any of it. "We gotta find another way."

Tripp sided with Leigh. "I bet y'all'd sing a different tune if your Dad was gonna whup you with a ruler."

Sis asked Leigh if she remembered Amu's bruises.

"Yeah."

"The deputy thinks he got them fighting with your uncle. That's going to look really bad to a jury. It might even get him convicted of murdering your uncle, unless we tell your parents that he got the bruises rescuing Mattie."

Leigh looked at us for the longest time before saying. "Yeah okay. Come on, y'all. Let's go inside."

We followed her inside. We were gonna catch holy hell, for sure. And even if Uncle Bud used the ruler on me, I'd still get the belt from Dad when I got home.

Uncle Bud was talking on the phone in the dining room. Because he was facing the wall he didn't see us gathering in a clump behind him. But Aunt Helen who'd been doing something at the sink had heard us come in. She told us to leave him alone.

He heard her and turned around. When he saw us he told the person he was talking to, "Let me call you back?"

He sat at the table. Us kids did too, except Mattie who stood by her dad's knee until he picked her up. She rested her head on his chest. Her eyes looked a little red, as though she'd been crying. Uncle Bud asked Leigh what we wanted.

"Will Amu go to prison?"

"In all likelihood."

"What if he didn't do it?"

Aunt Helen came over to sit with us, her gaze settling on

Leigh. "What is it that you're not telling us?"

Ignoring her mom, Leigh asked her dad, "Are they sure he killed Uncle Pete?"

"No, but he is a suspect."

"Then why does he have to go to jail?"

"Why all the questions? And why are you so concerned about a vagrant?"

"We feel sorry for him."

Aunt Helen gave us a very unsettling knowing look then asked Uncle Bud, "That Amu fellow could post bail, couldn't he?"

Mattie asked Uncle Bud why the jail was filling up with water.

Leigh snickered. Her mother gave her a warning look then told Mattie, "It's not that kind of bail, sweetie."

Mattie looked confused. I think she was about to ask her dad another question. Before she could, Leigh asked him, "How do you post bail?"

"You give the court some money and the judge lets you go free until your trial starts." Then he also told us not to get our hopes up.

Tripp asked him why.

"I doubt that Amu fellow has any money."

Mattie sat bolt upright in her dad's lap and looked him in the eyes. "He can have my allowance."

Uncle Bud smiled at her. "That's the sweetest thing I've heard all week, Missy. But I'm afraid your allowance wouldn't be nearly enough."

"Is it more than a million dollars?"

"Well, over a hundred anyway."

"Then I'll wish upon a star."

What do you say to a six-year-old who tells you that? Uncle Bud told her not to be disappointed if it didn't work."

"But it has to."

Jumping down off his lap, she announced, "I'll do it tonight" then headed for the back door.

Aunt Helen asked her where she was going."

"Outside to wait for the wishing star."

Aunt Helen told Tripp to go with her. We all went out and sat on the steps. I remembered thinking when I was little that wishing upon a star worked. I couldn't remember what had happened to ruin it for me. Mattie would be disappointed when her wish didn't work. I wondered if it would be the thing that ruined the magic for her.

Before we even got settled Sis lit into Leigh. "You said you'd tell your dad."

"I bet we'd have enough for Amu's bail if we put our money together."

Sis told her that just paying Amu's bail wouldn't prevent him from being convicted and sent to prison. Tripp said we should pay it if we could. That put me in a bad spot, especially when Leigh told us to go get our money so we could count it. I'd have to tell them I didn't have any. Then they'd ask why, and I'd have to tell them that I'd spent every cent I'd ever gotten for my allowance.

Sis told Leigh she'd left most of her money back home, which was a huge relief, because Sis saying it made it okay for me to say too, even if I didn't have any money back home. But then she ruined it by promising to ask our Mother for an advance on her allowance.

"Me too," I said, knowing full well that getting an advance on my allowance was about as likely as making a snowman right there in Florida in the dead of summer. At least it postponed the embarrassment until after we saw Mother. I hoped like hell I wouldn't see her any time soon.

COUNTING OUR MONEY

Just my luck, Mother came to Aunt Helen's for dinner that night. All I could think about during dinner was asking Mom for an advance on my allowance, knowing she'd say no, guaranteeing that I'd be embarrassed when Leigh asked me for my money. I was so upset I didn't have seconds of anything that night, not even the vanilla pudding. When mother left, Sis walked out to the car with her. I followed. It was do or die time.

Sis said, "Hey Mom?"

"Yes, Sarah."

"Can I have my allowance?"

"Yes dear."

"For the whole next month?"

Mom rummaged through her purse, finally taking out a twenty dollar bill which she handed to Sis.

Seeing how easy it had been for Sis, I thought, "why not? I've got nothing to lose." So I asked Mom for an advance on my allowance. She didn't say no right away, so I went for broke. "For the whole month?"

"Oh, Leonard, I don't think that's a good idea."

"Sure it is."

"You'll just spend it and ask for more."

"No I won't. I promise."

"I'm sorry, Leonard, but the answer's no."

Thinking my mistake had been to ask for the whole month, I asked for just the coming week's allowance.

"I gave you that last week."

I tried one last time as she was getting into the car. "Just one week. Please, Mom?"

She rolled her window down. "No, and that's final."

I grumbled a complaint.

"What was that, Leonard?"

"Nothing, Mom."

When she was too far away for them to hit her car I kicked up a spray of driveway stones then headed back to the house. As I walked past Sis she told me to wait there with her.

"Why?"

"Just do it."

I was glad I did, because when Mom's car disappeared Sis handed me two dollars. I thanked her. It wasn't much, but it would save me from total embarrassment. Sis had given me money without me even asking for it. It was the nicest thing anyone had done for me since almost forever.

On the way around back to rejoin our cousins Sis stopped and turned around and squinted at me, as though I had gone out of focus. I knew the look, and was pretty sure I knew what she was going to say. "You'd better pay me back."

We joined our cousins. Leigh knew Sis and I had asked Mom for our allowances. I wished I had more than two dollars. It didn't sound like much anymore, and to make things worse Sis suggested that Leigh keep a list of how much each of us gave. "That way you'll know how much to give us when we get our money back."

Sis barely had the words out before Mattie announced that she'd put in a million, thousand dollars.

Leigh smiled and shook her head. "How about seven dollars and change."

"That's almost a million," she said, which got snickers from Tripp and Leigh.

I dreaded the moment when Leigh would hold her hand

out for my money because little Mattie, who was half my age, had saved three times as much as I had, and even that wasn't mine. Tripp went inside for a piece of paper and pencil. So there it was. I was doomed. My cheapness would be written down and saved for all time.

Leigh didn't wait for Tripp to get back to ask for Sis' money. Then she asked for mine.

When I put the two dollars in her hand she frowned at it. "Well that does it. We don't have anywhere near a hundred dollars."

Mattie shoved Leigh hard enough from behind to knock her off balance.

"What was that for?"

Mattie screamed, "I hate you."

"Why? What'd I do?"

"It's all your fault."

Aunt Helen came to the back door. She'd heard Mattie yell and asked what she was upset about.

Leigh told her, "She's just mad because I wouldn't play patty-cake with her."

Mattie yelled, "Poopy liar."

Aunt Helen told Leigh, "It wouldn't kill you to let her choose the game once in a while."

"Come on, y'all," Leigh said, "let's go in and count it."

Leigh told us to wait for her in the dining room. She came back with a Chock-full-o-Nuts coffee can which she emptied on the table. The contents made a lot of noise but not much of a pile. Although I did see a few bills mixed in with the coins, when Leigh pressed the wrinkles out of them, I saw Lincoln's picture on most of them.

Aunt Helen asked her what the money was for.

"Amu's bail."

"That can't all be yours."

"We put our money together."

Thankfully, Leigh didn't tell them that almost none of it was mine, especially when Uncle Bud said it was an admirable thing to do. I felt like such a heel.

Aunt Helen counted out ten pennies, making a neat little stack out of them.

Mattie went over and stood next to her Mom, starting her own stack of pennies. "This is gonna be the biggest tower ever," she said, adding pennies quickly and carelessly, her tower growing more crooked with every penny added, until it looked like dishes stacked by The Cat in the Hat. It fell over knocking down one of Aunt Helen's stacks.

"Oh, poop," Mattie said, scrunching up her face in frustration then starting a new stack.

Aunt Helen made a stack of ten pennies then slid it in front of Mattie. "Make all of your stacks exactly this tall."

"How come?"

"If you do like I said, I'll show you a trick for counting coins."

Aunt Helen stacked the nickels, dimes, and quarters while Mattie did the pennies. All together our money added up to thirty-six dollars and change. Even if Mom had given me an advance on the whole next month it wouldn't have helped. Mattie asked her dad to pick her up. She curled up like a kitten and nuzzled her face against his neck.

Aunt Helen asked Uncle Bud, "What about asking Quintin to lower Amu's bail?"

"Quintin couldn't change Amu's bail even if he wanted to. That's set by the DA and the judge."

"What about those people who loan bail money?"

"Bail bondsmen? I doubt if they'd loan it to this Amu fellow."

"What about us?"

"The money would go to pay his bail. If Amu skipped out we'd have to pay it back."

Leigh asked her dad, "Isn't there anything we can do for him?"

Mattie stiffened up and turned so she and her dad were face to face. "Please, Daddy?"

Uncle Bud said he'd talk to the DA, but he said it with a frown. "Don't go getting your hopes up, Angel. He'll probably say no."

Then Uncle Bud told us to stay away from Amu. We nodded our heads, but did it without enthusiasm. I didn't think Amu would get out on bail.

That night, lying in bed waiting for sleep, I imagined the incident with Margo and Tommy Lee unfolding very differently, with Margo seeing Tommy Lee use his slingshot, and Mother staying indoors, and Margo thinking I was her hero. But I still couldn't find the right words to tell Margo I liked her, not even in my imagination.

And as for Tommy Lee, it didn't matter what I said to him, he always had the same answer. "Oh, yeah? You gonna make me?" So much for my imagination.

After breakfast the next morning, I helped Tripp collect garbage and muck out the horse stall while Sis helped Leigh feed the calves. We wasted the rest of the morning playing volleyball, well, trying to anyway. Leigh and I played against Sis and Tripp. We made them take Mattie because Sis could spike the ball without jumping. They put Mattie between them, and even though they set up some easy shots for her, she couldn't do it. When her frustration boiled over, we played tag instead.

After lunch Aunt Helen took us to Grandma Thurman's house and left us there with very clear instructions to stay outside. And she warned us at least three times not to bother Grandmother. Then she went to the hospital to sit with Grandfather so Grandmother could stay home and get some rest. Of course we couldn't force Grandmother to rest if she wanted to do something nice for us.

PAPA NEW GUINEA

Sis and my cousins and I were sitting cross-legged in the shade of a big live oak tree in Grandmother Thurman's back yard. Mattie answered a bunch of Sis' questions about school while Leigh picked on her about her answers. Tripp and I argued over who was the best batter ever, Mickey Mantle or Willie Mays. All that stopped when Grandmother brought us a pitcher of lemonade loaded with ice cubes and a tray with five aluminum glasses on it, each one a different color.

"Oh, I want the red one," Mattie said.

Grandmother asked us what we were plotting.

With deadly seriousness, Mattie announced, "We found an ogre living in Great Granddaddy's house."

"A real ogre?" Grandmother said, putting her hand on her chest. "I would like to hear all about that."

Leigh told Grandmother not to mind Mattie, that, "Ever since I read her a story about an ogre, she sees them all the time."

"Do not!"

"Now, Mattie," Grandmother said. "A well-behaved young lady doesn't yell at her sister."

"Well it's true," Mattie said, "cross my heart and hope to spit."

Grandmother held her hand out to Mattie. "Let's you and I take a walk."

Leigh said Mattie's name like a warning. Mattie looked back and stuck her tongue out at Leigh just before she and Grandmother disappeared around the corner of the house. That gave us plenty of time to wonder what Mattie was telling her before they reappeared at the far corner of the house; like whether or not Mattie told her about taking her out on the lake in a leaky rowboat. If she did, Grandmother would tell Aunt Helen, who would tell my mother. Then there'd be hell to pay.

When they came back Mattie sat in the grass with us. Grandmother stood nearby. I wondered if she remembered sitting in the grass when she was a kid.

"So," Grandmother said, "Mattie tells me you met a fellow named Amu, and that he's an ogre. Why do you suppose she thinks that?"

Tripp told her about Amu's scars. Leigh shook her head ever so slightly, a warning to Tripp.

Grandmother asked Mattie, "Is that right? Is it his scars that make him look like an ogre?"

Mattie nodded her head enthusiastically. Tripp told Grandmother they looked awful.

"I see," she said. "And how did he get them?"

"He told us a crocodile did it."

"I think you mean an alligator."

"I told him we didn't have no crocodiles around here."

Grandma frowned. "Any crocodiles, Tripp, we don't have any crocodiles around here."

"Isn't that what I said?"

Sis told Tripp that saying, "We don't have no crocodiles around here," was a double negative.

"Huh?"

"They should have taught you that in school."

Leigh made a funny sound as she tried to choke back a laugh. I guess she didn't dare make a wisecrack about Tripp in front of Grandmother. Grandmother asked Tripp what the scars looked like.

"Like there's ropes all over under his skin."

"Dear me, that must've hurt mightily."

Sis asked Grandmother what would cause scars like that.

"I don't know, but it reminds of something a friend once

told me. I'll go in and give her a call."

Grandmother headed toward the house. Leigh asked if she could go with her.

Mattie jumped up. "Ooh, ooh, can I come too?"

Grandmother shook her head, told us to wait there and drink our lemonade. She came back out a few minutes later to tell us her friend would be there soon, but it seemed like forever before we heard a car pull into the driveway out front.

We ran around the house in time to see a tiny old woman, mostly bones and loose wrinkly skin, get out of a car that looked even older than her, like the cars on the TV show, Elliot Ness. Leigh ran to Grandmother's door to ring the doorbell, easily beating the old woman who was moving as slow as molasses, which is how Mom described anything that moved extra slow.

When Grandmother answered the door, her friend said, "My but you do have a house full," in about the hoarsest voice I'd ever heard.

"They're my grandchildren."

Her friend said to us kids, "Your grandmother tells me you found a man with horrible scars."

I nodded my head. Leigh and Tripp both said, "Yes, ma'am." I felt my face get hot.

When Grandmother's friend warned her that some of what she had to say might not be appropriate for us children, Grandmother told us to find something to do out back and took her friend indoors.

Leigh whispered to Tripp, "Take Sarah and Mattie around back.

Then motioning to me with her finger to follow her, she crouched down and snuck in behind some bushes under Grandmother's living room windows. I did the same, kneeling next to her.

If we were quiet and no cars went by, we could hear what Grandmother's friend said. "Years ago one of our Methodist missionaries, a Father Menendez, brought a boy back with him from the jungles of Papa New Guinea in Southeast Asia.

111

Menendez went there hoping to convert one of the river tribes.

"While he was there he heard rumors about a cruel pagan ritual that left young boys horribly scared. The next time he heard about them performing the ceremony he burst in to stop it. Unfortunately for the boy the ceremony was almost over, so the boy had already endured the worst of the pain, and the tribe refused to finish the ceremony after a foreigner had interrupted it. The boy was shunned by his tribe after that because he hadn't achieved manhood. Father Menendez brought the boy home with him so he wouldn't have to endure the shame."

Grandmother asked her what they did to the boys.

"During the ceremony an elder from the tribe cuts the boy with a sharp bamboo sliver, re-cutting each wound repeatedly. Before it's over the boy will be cut more than a thousand times."

"My God. That's barbaric."

"Oh that's not the end of it. The elder puts a paste made from ash and river mud into the cuts with a feather."

"To help the healing?"

"To cause infection."

"Oh dear me," Grandmother said. "Why in heaven's name would he do that?"

"Because the more infected the cuts get, the bigger the scars will be, and the more the boy's skin will resemble a crocodile's."

"And that's the desired result?"

"The tribe believes that the scars make the boys kindred spirits of the crocodile."

"Anyone with doubts about the advantages of civilization needs to hear that story."

If that had happened to Amu, he had gone through more pain in one day that I had in my whole life. I'd grown up believing that life was fair, that everybody got pretty much the same amount of good and bad, but after hearing what Amu had suffered I realized I'd been terribly wrong. The world was a much scarier place after that.

Grandma asked her friend how something so cruel had

gotten started.

"It's an ancient ceremony based on their belief that the crocodile is the most powerful creature in the jungle, and that its power is absorbed into their bodies while they recover, or some such nonsense."

"Deliberately causing infections in a jungle environment is incredibly foolhardy."

"Before the ceremony the boys are taught sacred myths and taboos, and they're told they'll die in the spirit house if they break any of the taboos. It's their explanation for why some of the boys die."

"What ever happened to the boy?"

"Father Menendez hoped that showing his congregation the boy's scars would convince them of the need for more missionary work in New Guinea."

"Did it work?"

"No. He was sent to the orient."

"And the boy?"

"Menendez left him here in someone's care, but he ran away and was never seen again."

GRANDMOTHER OFFERS TO HELP

When we heard Grandmother's friend say she was leaving, we crawled out of the bushes quick like bunnies. We were standing out in the yard away from the house trying very hard to look innocent when Grandmother came out to walk her friend to her car.

Grandmother looked at us with suspicion. I wondered why until I noticed the sand and black dirt on Leigh's pants from kneeling in the bushes. I didn't look much better. Leigh saw me brushing it off and did the same.

Tripp and Sis and Mattie must have heard the car door because they came from the back yard to join us. I expected we'd get a scolding from Grandmother, or at the very least some questions after she waved goodbye to her friend. Instead she asked us what we knew about Amu.

Leigh told her that they arrested him for killing their Uncle Pete. Grandmother took in a quick deep breath and put her hand on her chest. Leigh told her that we put all our money together for his bail.

"Why on earth would you do that if he killed your uncle?"

"Because he didn't."

She frowned, asked, "Are you sure about that?"

That got her five nodding heads and a jumble of mumbled,

"Yes, ma'ams."

After giving Leigh the long silent lie detector stare that parents use, Grandmother said, "Is there something you're not telling me?"

Leigh said, "No, ma'am," but the way she said it, it sounded more like a question than an answer.

"I see, well where did you kids get enough money for Amu's bail?"

"We didn't."

Before Grandmother went inside she told us she couldn't promise anything, but that she might be able to help.

Mattie jumped up and down and clapped her hands. I bet people in the next state heard her screech, "Yippee." When she saw us cringe she giggled then did it again.

We finished the afternoon back at their place with more than a little arguing about what to do next. That night, lying in bed wondering if Grandmother's friend was right about how Amu got his scars, I thought about how painful a sliver was then tried to imagine a thousand of them.

Aunt Helen's announcement the next morning at breakfast, that we had to go into town with her for groceries earned her a collective groan from my cousins. Tripp asked her why.

"Because your father will want dinner tonight when he gets home."

"But why can't we stay here?"

"Because I don't trust you to behave."

"We'll be good, won't we, Leigh?"

Aunt Helen gave him one of those "I know better" looks, the kind my mother was always giving me, where she purses her lips and turns her head to the side then rolls her eyes."

But then Sis asked if she could stay to practice the piano and Aunt Helen said "Sure."

That presented an opportunity which Leigh recognized immediately. "Sarah will make sure we don't get into trouble, won't you, Sarah?"

Sis frowned. Aunt Helen asked her if she minded keeping an eye on us. I know Sis hated the idea, but she agreed to do it anyway, because it's what a grownup would do, and Sis was practically a grownup. Aunt Helen told us to mind Sis and stay in the house, which was tons better than riding all the way into town and back in a hot crowded car, not to mention the long boring walk through the grocery store.

After warning us to behave one last time, Aunt Helen left. Sis suggested we play "Life" while she played the piano. Mattie said she didn't know how and suggested we all play "Chutes and Ladders" instead. Tripp objected. Sis told us to vote on it. Leigh and Tripp and I voted for "Life". Mattie crossed her arms and pouted.

Sis patted the seat on the chair next to her. "If you want, we can play together, Mattie." So much for her practicing the piano. But it was nice of Sis. It was also wasted because it didn't end Mattie's pouting. Sis tried again. At least I think it was my sister. It looked like her. Anyway, Sis told Mattie she could move the little car for them. Mattie stormed out of the room. Leigh told Tripp to follow her and make sure she didn't leave the house. He sighed and rolled his eyes then followed her.

I grabbed the little red car. Leigh told Sis she was the banker then grabbed the white car. While Sis handed out our $10,000 starting money, Leigh and I put people pegs in our cars.

A minute or two later Tripp came back. "She's lying on the couch pretending to sleep."

Sis told him to choose a car. He looked at my red one and frowned then took the blue one. Sis took the yellow one. When she finished setting up the money we each spun the wheel to see what the order of players would be. I ended up going last and didn't land on any of the good career squares, like doctor or lawyer, which meant I'd probably end up in the poorhouse.

Later I landed on an "Adopt Twin Sons" square and was putting two blue pegs in my car when I heard loud clomping sounds coming from the hallway. We all stopped playing and watched the door. I couldn't imagine what was coming.

Mattie appeared in the doorway wearing a big floppy hat and a clump of necklaces, some of them hanging down almost to the floor. She had on grownup-size, high-heeled shoes, which explained the clomping sound.

With her right hand on her hip so her elbow stuck out, she sauntered into the room, swinging her hips and her elbow in an exaggerated swishing motion the way Olive Oyl did to impress Bluto. With lipstick smeared around her mouth and bright pink circles on her cheeks, she reminded me of a carnival clown. I had all I could do not to laugh.

Obviously struggling to hold back a laugh, Leigh choked out, "Oh man, you've really done it now."

"Have not," Mattie said, defiantly.

"If Momma catches you wearing her clothes, she is gonna whup you good."

Mattie stuck her chin out. "Momma said I could wear them."

Leigh called her a liar.

"Hey you guys," Sis said. "Your mother asked me to keep an eye on you. If we don't get Mattie cleaned up I'm going to be in real trouble."

Leigh asked Sis if she knew how to get makeup off.

Sis shook her head.

Leigh rolled her eyes then led a squirming Mattie out of the room by her arm. Tripp and Sis followed them. They didn't need my help getting the makeup off, but with nothing better to do, I went along to watch the spectacle. Leigh took Mattie to their parent's room.

Leigh used a tissue to wipe the lipstick off. That got some of it off and smeared the rest. Aunt Helen would notice it for sure. Leigh used another tissue to wipe the pink stuff off of Mattie's cheeks, rubbing them so hard she got an "Oowie" and some serious squirming from Mattie.

That earned Mattie a slap on the butt, and Tripp a scolding. "Hold her still, will ya?"

Sis left the room and came back two minutes later with

a wet washcloth, which she handed to Leigh. Rubbing gently at first, Leigh was soon back to scrubbing poor Mattie's cheeks, squishing them as though she was kneading bread dough, which got Mattie crying. When Leigh gave up, Mattie had one bright pink cheek from the makeup and one bright red cheek from the scrubbing. Both of her eyes were smudged with runny black stuff and she was bawling.

Leigh yelled, "Stupid girl."

"I am not stupid."

"You'd better stop your crying and stand still, because if we don't get this makeup off, Momma's gonna whup you so hard you won't be able to sit for a week."

Tripp, who like the rest of us had been looking at the door every few seconds, as though he expected his mother to suddenly appear, suggested that Leigh take the jewelry and clothes off first.

"Yeah, good idea, Tripp, 'cause this sure isn't working. You take the clothes off. I'll put them away."

Tripp told Mattie to put her arms up. She sort of did. He pulled Mattie's arms up straight then slid the dress off. Leigh tried to put it on a hanger but the straps kept slipping off the ends of it.

"Give it to me," Sis said, crossing the straps so they wouldn't slip off the hanger. She told Leigh, "If we're not careful she'll know someone was messing with her things."

"Huh?"

"It looks like your mother puts the clothes she uses most near the front and her good dresses in the back of her closet."

"Fine, you hang it up. I gotta get this jewelry off of her."

When Dana started barking Leigh told Tripp to go see if it was their mother. Then she attempted to get the mass of necklaces over Mattie's head without getting them tangled in her hair.

Trip came back breathing heavily. "Momma just parked the car. She'll be here any second."

Leigh handed Sis the necklaces and told her to put them

118

away quick. Sis did not look happy.

Then Leigh grabbed Mattie by the collar. "You're coming with me. The rest of you go to the playroom."

Leigh pulled Mattie to the bathroom by her arm. Sis and Tripp and I barely made it to the playroom before Aunt Helen showed up. Sis wasn't playing the piano. Tripp and I stood there looking surprisingly guilty considering that, for a change, we weren't. She asked where Leigh and Mattie were. Tripp told her. She frowned at us then left.

I heard her knock on the bathroom door and ask, "Leigh, have you got Mattie in there?"

Moments later I heard Aunt Helen yell, "What in God's name have you two been up to?"

I heard a loud smack then Mattie screaming.

Sis said, "Poor little kid."

Tripp told her not to worry, that, "Momma doesn't spank Mattie near as hard as she does me."

As usual, Sis and I got off Scott-free, which I thought was fair for a change.

AMU GETS OUT ON BAIL

When the phone rang halfway through dinner Aunt Helen told Leigh to answer it. She told her dad it was for him.

After Uncle Bud answered the phone he said, "Is that so?" then, "I suppose he could stay at Grandad's cabin if he doesn't have anywhere else to go."

He came back to the table frowning. Aunt Helen asked him what was wrong.

"Someone paid Amu's bail. Quintin's bringing him out to the cabin."

Mattie clapped her hands and yelled, "Yippee!"

Aunt Helen told her to shush then asked Uncle Bud who paid it.

"I don't know. Whoever it was sent cash and a note saying it was for Amu's bail. No signature on the note. No return address either."

Looking at us kids with suspicion, Aunt Helen asked if we knew anything about it. We shook our heads, told her we didn't.

She asked Uncle Bud, "Why the frown?"

"Quintin ran a trace on this Amu character. Apparently he spent some time at Shady Brook."

Aunt Helen inhaled loud enough for me to hear. Leigh asked her what Shady Brook was.

"An asylum. Now hush while I talk to your father."

120

Mattie asked, "What's a "sylum, Mom?"

Aunt Helen asked Uncle Bud why Amu had been there.

"Quintin didn't say. But the point is, Amu could be dangerous."

"That does it," Aunt Helen said, "you kids stay away from him."

She got a chorus of feeble-sounding "yes, ma'ams."

I had no doubt Leigh would find a reason to go see Amu. And she'd ask us who wanted to go with her. I was already in enough trouble for one summer, but I'd say yes anyway so I'd have another adventure to tell Margo about. I bet Tommy Lee couldn't top bad guys chasing us at the swamp or us looking for a killer.

Leigh asked her dad if Quintin had said anything about the men stealing water.

"That's Mr. Mayville to you, young lady."

"Did Mr. Mayville say anything about those men we saw stealing water?"

"It wasn't them."

"How does he know?"

"They had alibis for the night Pete was killed."

Mattie asked her dad what an alibi was.

"Someone said those men were someplace else when Pete was killed.

At the same time Mattie asked him, "Does Amu have one of those things?" Tripp asked him, "How do they know when Pete was killed?"

"I called and talked to Pete before breakfast Tuesday."

Mattie said, "Dad," in a drawn out, singsong way.

"Let me answer Tripp first, Princess."

Mattie crossed her arms and pouted while Uncle Bud told Tripp, "When Pete didn't show up for work Wednesday, I called him. His wife said Pete didn't come home Tuesday night, so it must have happened that night."

Not to be ignored, Mattie said, "Ahem," loudly.

Uncle Bud smiled at her. "Okay, Mattie, it's your turn."

121

"Does Amu have one of those things?"

"One of what things?"

"You know, where someone says you're someplace else."

"You mean an alibi?"

That got a big, serious nod from Mattie.

"No, princess, he doesn't."

"Then let's get him one."

Tripp grinned. Leigh made another choking sound trying to stifle a laugh. Mattie stuck her tongue out. Aunt Helen told them to behave.

Mattie said, "Can we, Daddy."

"Can we what, princess?"

"Get him one of those things."

"His lawyer will look for someone who can give him an alibi."

"I can do it."

Aunt Helen gave Leigh and Tripp a threatening look before they even had a chance to laugh.

Uncle Bud told Mattie, "I'm sorry, princess, but it has to be a grownup."

"No fair," she said, slouching in her chair with her arms folded and her bottom lip pouched out.

"Okay, that's enough," Aunt Helen said. "I want y'all outside, now."

All of us except Mattie met out at the bridge. She came out a few minutes later carrying a doll and sat in the grass nearby singing something to herself while she fussed with the doll, trying to get it to sit up in the grass by itself. It kept falling over, like in one of those old silent comedies I saw where they tried to get a passed-out drunk to sit up. I would've given up, but somehow she persuaded the thing to stay upright.

Leigh said to Sis, "I saw a Nancy Drew book on your cot."

"I like her books."

"What would she do?"

"Nancy Drew is make-believe."

"Yeah, but if she was real, what would she do?"

"Mostly she looks for clues and people who have motives."

Tripp told us about a Sherlock Holmes movie he saw where Sherlock found the killer just from the mud on the guy's boots. "He even knew where in England the mud came from. Can Nancy Drew do that?"

"Forget that, Sarah" Leigh said. "Tell us what to do about Amu?"

"Well, that deputy thinks your uncle and Amu got into a fight after your uncle saw Amu's fire from the Williston Cutoff."

"So"

"So your Dad doesn't think it's possible to see a fire at your great granddad's place from the Williston Cutoff."

"So?"

"If you could prove it. That would mean that Amu and your uncle didn't get into a fight."

"I could start a fire at the cabin then go to the Cutoff to look for it?"

"Yep."

"But suppose I did start a fire there and I couldn't see it from the Cutoff, do you think Quintin would believe me?"

"I bet your dad would, and if he didn't you could show him. And he could tell Quintin."

Tripp shook his head. "It takes a whole day just to get there and back. And to prove you can't see the fire, we'd have to walk the whole length of the Cutoff."

"Then we'll take Peanut," Leigh said.

I asked her what Peanut was.

"Our horse."

I could've guessed what was coming next. Sure enough Leigh asked us who wanted to go with her. "There's room for two on Peanut."

I thought Mattie had been too busy playing with her doll to hear us, but her little arm went up so fast it was a blur. "Ooh, ooh, take me."

After telling Mattie, "No," so forcefully, it sounded like a scolding, Leigh asked me if I wanted to go. I told her I would because I didn't want Leigh telling Margo I'd chickened out of something.

"Then it's settled," she said, "we'll go tonight. Same as before, Leonard, put your clothes back on after Mom turns out the hall light. I'll come get you when the coast is clear."

TROUBLE AT THE WILLISTON CUTOFF

To stay awake until Leigh came for me I thought about Margo, pretending once again to be her hero, which once again, ended in disappointment. Then I tried thinking about being home with my friends exploring the gorge near my house and looking for crayfish. But how much time can you spend daydreaming about catching crayfish when you've already done it a hundred times? So I was stuck listening to Tripp snore.

I woke up to a hand over my mouth and Leigh shaking me. And yeah, the hand was a good idea because I would've screamed otherwise. Like the time before, we tiptoed out sock-footed, carrying our shoes from the laundry then sat on the back steps to put them on. After a fast walk through two pastures Dana came racing from the barn to join us, wiggling and barking and nuzzling Leigh's hand.

Leigh snapped a branch off of a low-hanging willow near the barn. She told me we'd need it if we wanted to get back before the sun came up. I asked her why.

"You'll see," she said, walking on ahead.

At the barn door she handed me a flashlight. "Hold this for me while I put the saddle on him."

I panned the light around the inside of the barn. It looked like a house of horrors, held together by the cobwebs that covered every inch of it. But in spite of all the webs and all of dead bugs in them, there had to be a million flies buzzing around us.

"Hey," Leigh said, "how about a little light over here?"

I got a good look at Peanut then. I wasn't especially worried about riding him because I'd taken horse riding lessons back home, and because he was an ancient dapple-gray swayback. I figured our biggest problem would be getting him to move.

But even though Leigh gave Peanut the carrot she had in her back pocket and patted his face, he shook his head violently when she slipped the bridle over his head. All of the horses I'd ridden back home had come with a bridle and saddle already in place. I had no idea that putting a bridle on could actually be dangerous.

After coaxing Peanut out of his stall Leigh handed me the reins and told me, "Don't let go of them, no matter what."

Peanut shook his head and tried to back away, pulling back on the reins so quick and so hard he nearly yanked them out of my hands. Leigh swatted him on the rump. Dana barked at him. Peanut reared.

While he tried unsuccessfully to stomp on my feet and kick Dana, Leigh threw a saddle on him. She managed to get the cinch strap in place and tighten it in spite of the dance she and Dana and I were doing to keep our feet out from under Peanut's hooves. Leigh pointed at a step stool and told me to bring it.

Peanut reared and snorted and balked as Leigh led him out of the barn. Outside, she talked soothingly to him and stroked his neck, which eased the kicking and balking, but only a little. Leigh set the stool on the ground near him then in one smooth motion put her left foot in the stirrup and swung her right leg up over the saddle, making it look easy, even with Peanut dancing the whole time.

Taking her left foot out of the stirrup she said, "Your turn."

My stomach flip-flopped like a fish out of the water. Peanut did a dance, moving away from me. I moved the stool closer.

"That's as still as I can hold him," Leigh said.

Peanut moved again. I moved the stool again.

"Just jump on. And hold on tight or he'll throw you off."

I slipped my left foot in the stirrup, then pulling hard on the pummel with my left hand and the back of the saddle with my right hand, I swung my right leg over Peanut's back and grabbed Leigh's waist. Peanut turned his head back and tried to bite my leg. Leigh slapped his nose. The dancing and balking got worse. She gave him a kick. He started walking.

I was hugely uncomfortable sitting in the saddle with her because I kept sliding down the back of it into Leigh, which pulled my underwear tight, pinching my privates. And if that wasn't bad enough, Peanut's saddle blanket smelled like rotting hay, horse-sweat, and old clothes that had been kept in a hot attic.

Leigh told me to hold on tight then swatted Peanut's rear with the willow switch. You'd have thought his butt was on fire the way he took off. I held on to Leigh for dear life. Peanut broke into a full gallop. Dana ran alongside us barking, making enough noise to wake the dead.

After a while Leigh slowed Peanut to a trot. You know how sometimes you get a spanking that doesn't hurt too badly, then you hear your dad telling your mom that his heart just wasn't in it? Well bouncing on that saddle was worse than a spanking from Dad when his heart was in it.

Leigh slowed Peanut to a walk when her great grandfather's cabin came into view. Dana ran on ahead, almost to the cabin. He barked until Amu came out and stood in the dog trot then ran back to us. With a kick to the ribs Leigh got Peanut to trot the rest of the way to the cabin. She stopped him ten feet from the dogtrot.

Amu asked what we were doing out so late.

Leigh told him to build a fire, "a big one."

"It's too hot for a fire."

"It'll keep you out of jail."

"I'm already out of jail."

"I'll do it myself if you won't."

After warning us to stay clear of the swamp he walked toward the fire pit. Leigh swatted Peanut with the willow switch. He took off, working himself up to a gallop, but it wasn't long before he slowed to a trot again. I told Leigh that it didn't hurt near as much when he galloped.

"He's an old horse and it's a long ride to the cutoff. He'll die if we push him to hard," so it was a long butt-pounding ride.

Leigh slowed Peanut to a walk again when we came to a rough dirt road lined with trees on both sides. Leigh twisted around in the saddle to tell me, "This is the Williston Cutoff."

Then we began a long slow walk looking through the trees for Amu's fire. After staring into the trees for the longest time without seeing anything, she stopped Peanut and told me to shush. We sat there for I don't know how long. I neither saw nor heard a thing until Leigh muttered an obscenity. She kicked Peanut. He trotted. I swore under my breath, which didn't help my butt one bit. We hadn't gone far when she stopped Peanut again. I asked her why.

"Don't you hear em?"

I shook my head.

She pointed into the darkness, said in a loud whisper, "Over that way" then turned Peanut in the direction she'd pointed and kicked him.

He walked. I thanked my lucky stars. It wasn't long before I saw the swamp through the trees, the place where monsters waited below the surface to eat me, and slithery venomous things with three inch fangs waited in the woods around it to bite me. And if you could believe Amu, there was something even worse than snakes or gators in there.

Leigh stopped Peanut under a willow tree near the water's edge. The same two men who had chased us the night we went fishing stood no farther away than I could throw a stone. I whispered in Leigh's ear, told her we should go back.

For some reason Peanut decided right then, on his own,

to walk out into the open toward the lake. Leigh yanked on his reins so hard he whinnied. From then on it was Déjà vu; the two men looking in our direction, one of them pointing at us, then both of them running.

Leigh yanked the reins hard to the left then swatted Peanut with the willow branch. He turned around so slowly it was maddening. When she swatted him again he started to trot. She swatted him again and he galloped. She let him have it a fourth time, but he wouldn't go any faster. I heard a truck roar to life. Night turned into day a moment later when we were caught in the truck's headlights.

I looked back. The truck wasn't far behind us. I could hit a baseball farther and I played second string ball. I told Leigh they were going to catch us. Peanut turned toward the glossy black expanse of the lake. Try as she might Leigh couldn't turn him away from the water. I barely had time to feel scared before Peanut plunged into the swamp.

When the water reached his belly Peanut made a sudden left turn back toward shore. Not expecting him to do that, I wasn't holding on as tightly as I should have. When my weight shifted hard to the right my knee buckled. By then my weight had shifted too far to recover.

I had a moment of disbelief, the kind you have when you realize something bad is happening to you and there's nothing you can do about it. For one freakish moment I felt weightless. Then my legs went to the left with Peanut. The rest of me went to the right. I twisted and grabbed for Leigh or the saddle but got a handful of air.

I held my arms out to break my fall. My hands slapped the water first. Then a cool wetness raced up my arms as puke-green muck rushed toward my face. My belly-flop was a ten-pointer. And dumb me, I'd forgotten to hold my breath so I gagged on a mouthful of water with chunky stuff in it that was too gross to think about. I spit and coughed and accidently took in another mouthful. To get my face out of the water I pushed with my arms. Muck oozed up between my fingers as they sunk into the lake bottom. I got my legs under me and pushed. My feet sunk up to my shins before I raised my head above the water. Knowing I'd swallowed some of the oatmeally-looking stuff floating on the surface, I gagged. I gagged again then spit until I had no spit left then dry-heaved.

I was a car length from shore with wet clothes clinging to my arms and legs when I realized to my horror that a gator might be about to clamp its teeth around my leg and drag me under to make a meal out of me. If one was nearby, the noise I'd made flailing would definitely have gotten its attention, and I'd never see it coming.

The gator terror faded after I made it to the water's edge and flopped down on the mossy bank. I sat up and looked for Leigh and Peanut but didn't see them. I did see truck lights through the tree line.

Then I remembered Leigh telling me how a gator had come out of the lake and grabbed their miniature poodle ten feet from the water, and any dog, even a little one, can run faster than I ever could. Even though there might be a rattler waiting for me in the brush but I decided being bitten by a snake was a dang sight better than being eaten by an alligator.

And that wasn't my only problem. I had no idea which direction to go to get back to my cousins' house. And the truck was getting closer, close enough for me to hear the rumble of its engine. I lay down and rolled under a bush. The truck stopped so close to me I smelled exhaust fumes.

I heard two doors close. When I saw the crazy zigzag patterns of a flashlight beam searching for me I rolled farther under the bushes, and while I was lying there, my mind, which had never been very helpful in panic situations, conjured up the image of a snake-den under me. As much as I wanted to scream when I felt something touch my leg, I didn't. A lifetime later I heard the truck doors slam. Then I heard the men drive away. I couldn't get out of those bushes fast enough.

Standing on the lakeshore I took stock of my predicament: the two men might come back; I didn't know which direction my cousin's house was; I still had swamp grit in my teeth, damp slimy clothes clinging to me, and I reeked of swamp water.

I had learned some survival skills as a Cub Scout, but building a lean to, or starting a fire without matches, wouldn't be much help this time. Then I heard a dog bark somewhere off beyond the tree line. Moments later Leigh came out of the trees riding Peanut. I waved. She didn't see me. I didn't dare yell so I ran toward them. I was maybe halfway to her when she spotted me.

She stopped Peanut next to me and took her foot out of the stirrup. Wrapping her right arm around Peanut's neck she held her left hand out to me. In spite of us locking our arms together, getting into the saddle was a real struggle with Peanut dancing.

When I slid in behind her, she said, "Oowee, Leonard, you sure do stink."

"It tastes worse than it smells."

She told me to hold on, that we had to hurry, and, "If you fall off again you won't have soft water to land in."

I pleaded with her to let Peanut walk.

"I'm sorry, Leonard, but we have to get back before Dad gets up."

On our way to the barn, Leigh stopped at the cabin to tell Amu he could put the fire out. He looked me over then made a face. "Went for a swim, did ya?" As we rode away he yelled to our backsides, "Didn't I tell you to stay away from the swamp?"

Leigh waved to him without looking back. Back at the barn, after she put Peanut and the tack away, she told me to follow her. She led me to a watering trough and told me to climb in. There was cattle drool floating in it. I shook my head.

"If Momma gets a whiff of you, she'll know we were at the lake."

I hesitated.

"When you're done you can rinse your face off under the spigot, but we've gotta hurry."

I climbed in.

"Lower."

"Not my head."

"Your head stinks."

I closed my eyes and held my nose and ducked under, gagging at the thought of cow spit on my face. When I came out Leigh cranked the hand pump for me so I could rinse off. We ran back to my cousins' house with Leigh leading the way and me slogging along behind in wet clothes and squeaky shoes.

When we got to the fence at their back yard Leigh stopped to tell me, "Take your clothes off."

I shook my head.

"Undies too."

"Huh?"

"You can't take them inside."

I told her I'd put them in the dirty clothes.

"They're too wet."

"Then what do I do with them?"

"Give them to me. I'll hide them in the shed. We'll rinse them out tomorrow with the hose so they don't stink so much. When they dry we can put them in the hamper."

I stood behind a bush to undress, tossing my clothes over it, not leaving the safety of it until I saw Leigh go indoors. Then I had to go in and make the long scary naked walk on my tiptoes to Tripp's room. The idea of getting caught by her parents was scary enough, but the thought of them catching me naked was scarier than all of the horror houses at all of the county fairs all put together. Clean underwear and pajamas never felt as good as they did that night.

MATTIE SEES A DRAGON

Next day, all of us kids went to the hospital with Aunt Helen to see Grandfather Thurman. On the walk in from the parking lot Sis and Aunt Helen stopped to gawk at the flowers planted near the entrance. Carrying the paper sack full of things to do that she always brought with her to the hospital, Mattie nagged Leigh about reading Charlotte's Web to her. Lagging behind so we wouldn't get caught in girl talk, Tripp and I stopped to look at a shiny red Corvette. I guess we lost track of time, because Aunt Helen yelled to us to hurry up.

When I looked in her direction I saw Scruffy two parking spaces away leaning on a car reading a magazine and smoking a cigarette. It was just a Ford Falcon, a real grandmother's car, but it had an air scoop on the hood like a dragster. The edges of the hole cut through the hood looked ragged, as though a kid had done it. And the dull primer-red paint job didn't match the vomit-green color of the car, which reminded me of the scum on my cousin's swamp. But that didn't matter, because with that stupid-looking air scoop no one was going to notice that the colors didn't match.

Mattie and Leigh were just then walking past Scruffy. For some reason Mattie stopped right in front of him. She stood there and stared at him. He looked at her without so much as a smile or a "Hi kid."

Realizing she'd walked on ahead without Mattie, Leigh hurried back and grabbed her hand and led her toward the hospital.

Aunt Helen yelled, "Come on, Tripp, we haven't got all day."

From the time he and I passed Scruffy until we got inside I had the feeling of being watched, and it didn't go away until we took the hallway to the right because until then Scruffy could still see us through the all-glass front entrance of the hospital. Walking fast to keep up with Aunt Helen and Sis, I didn't get a chance to tell my cousins about seeing Scruffy the last time we came to see Grandfather.

After we'd all said "hi" to Grandfather and held his hand for a minute or two, which seemed kinda weird, Aunt Helen told us kids to go to the waiting room. Well, except for Sis, unless she wanted to go with us. Leigh asked her to. When we got there Sis asked her why.

"Go ahead, Mattie, tell 'em what you told me."

Mattie pointed at the window. "That man out there has Uncle Pete's dragon."

Tripp asked her what she was talking about.

Standing with her little fists on her hips, she looked like an angry miniature grownup. "Uncle Pete's dragon, silly."

Leigh told her to keep her voice down.

Tripp looked at us and shrugged his shoulders then said to Mattie, "Momma's right, you've gotta stop making things up."

Mattie stomped her foot. "I am not making this up."

Sis said, "I think she saw something. The question is what."

Saying the words slowly, as though that would clear up our confusion and make it a fact, Mattie repeated herself, "I told you. That man has Uncle Pete's dragon."

We went to the window for a look. When that didn't clear it up for us, Leigh said, "Come on, Leonard. We'll go see for ourselves."

Sis shook her head. "I don't think that's a good idea."

"Why?"

"He looks like trouble."

"You're as bad as Tripp. Hell, I bet he doesn't even notice us."

A few minutes later I walked out of the building with Leigh. I was nervous and she was wrong – Scruffy did notice us. He stared right at us as we walked to within one parked car of him. But I didn't see a dragon.

When we crossed to the sidewalk on the other side of the road Scruffy yelled to us, "You kids ain't fooling anybody."

Halfway back to the entrance, I glanced at him. He was still watching us. It gave me the willies. Tripp and Sis and Mattie came to meet us in the hallway outside the waiting room. Tripp asked Leigh if we saw a dragon.

"She made it up."

"Did not," Mattie said, scowling at her sister, her little arms folded across her chest.

Leigh told her to keep her voice down.

"You can't boss me around."

"Cain too."

Sis told Mattie to pretend Tripp was Scruffy and touch him where she saw the dragon.

Without hesitation, Mattie poked Tripp's belt buckle. "Right there."

"Well that explains it," Sis said. "His belt buckle is right at eye level for Mattie. That's why she saw it and you didn't.

Tripp told us that his uncle had a belt buckle with a funny-looking picture on it; "Kind of like a lion standing on its hind legs with its front legs up in the air. He got it for being some kind of engineer in the war."

Sis asked him if it might look like a dragon to Mattie.

He shrugged his shoulders. "I don't know. Maybe."

Sis told Leigh that we had to tell her parents.

"Why?"

"Not in front of Mattie."

Leigh sent Mattie to ask their mother how long it would be before we went home.

"Why can't Tripp do it?"

"Do you want me to tell Momma that you cussed?"

After saying, "Oh, poopy," Mattie stomped off toward Grandfather's room.

Leigh asked Sis what was so bad that she couldn't say it in front of Mattie.

"If the buckle she saw was your uncle's, then either that man out there killed him or he got the buckle from the killer."

Leigh rolled her eyes. "Or Mattie made it up to get some attention."

"Mattie stopped right in front of him and stared at it. If that guy is the killer, he'll be worried about her telling somebody."

I told Sis what Scruffy had said about not fooling anyone.

"Well, that settles it."

"Settles what? Leigh asked.

"He knows that we know, which means that Mattie's in danger."

Leigh walked away shaking her head, mumbling, "Y'all are nuts."

Tripp asked Sis, "You really think Mattie's in danger?"

"I think we all are."

I heard a faint moan from Tripp. "Really? All of us?"

Sis nodded her head, and she was smarter than the rest of us put together.

UNCLE PETE'S DRAGON

When Mattie came back she asked Sis to read Charlotte's Web to her instead of Leigh. Sis agreed. Leigh flipped through a National Geographic magazine. Tripp and I stood at the window checking out the cars in the parking lot.

After a while I saw the same nurse I'd seen talking to Scruffy walk out of the hospital. I called Sis and Leigh over, and told them to hurry. Mattie came with them. I told them to watch Scruffy and the nurse. When the nurse got to Scruffy's car she stopped. Scruffy said something to her then they both looked back at the hospital. I swear they looked right at us. They left together in the puke green Ford with the silly-looking hood scoop. Sis said she didn't like the looks of it. I told her I didn't either; that the hood-scoop made it just about the dumbest-looking car ever.

"No silly. I didn't mean the car. I don't like seeing the nurse who was talking to Aunt Helen leaving with the guy Mattie says has her uncle's belt buckle."

Leigh came back, asked us what the fuss was all about.

Tripp told her about the nurse and Scruffy.

Leigh shook her head. "I still say Mattie did it for the attention."

"Did not."

"Did so."

Sis shushed them because people in the waiting room were staring at us. That gave me a chance to tell them about Scruffy's kid being mean to me. But I only got as far as telling them, "Scruffy's kid was here," before Sis told my cousins, "We have to tell your parents about that guy."

Leigh snickered at her. "You think they'd believe us?"

"Why wouldn't they?"

"You really want to tell them we know who killed Uncle Pete because Mattie saw a dragon on some guy's belt?"

Tripp said, "If you're so smart, Leigh, you tell us what we should do."

"Ask that guy where he got the buckle."

Sis asked her if she serious.

"Sure."

It sounded like trouble to me. Leigh asked if any of us had a better idea.

Sis asked her how she planned to find his house. "You don't even know his name."

Leigh asked me how old I thought Scruffy's kid was.

"I don't know, high school I guess."

Leigh said she'd ask her mother for the Nurse's name. "My friend's sister goes to the high school. She might recognize the name, might even know his first name and where he lives."

Sis made a face, said, "Even if that guy knows what happened to your uncle, why would he tell you?"

"I don't know. I'll think of something." Then looking around at each of us, one at a time, daring us to say no, Leigh asked, "Well, who's going with me?"

Mattie's hand was up in a blink. "I am."

Leigh grinned, told Tripp. "See, Mattie's not a pansy."

"Yeah? Well how do you plan to get to his house?"

It only took her a second to figure that out. "I'll take the bus from Grandma Thurman's next time we're there."

Instead of waiting to be asked, I told Leigh I'd go. That way I could tell Margo I volunteered.

"See, Tripp, Leonard's not afraid."

Tripp and Sis looked at each other. Tripp shrugged his shoulders.

Sis rolled her eyes, said, "I still think it's a bad idea," but agreed to go anyway, which was good, because I liked having a strong guy like Tripp, and an almost-grownup like Sis with us, just in case something bad happened.

Later while Leigh and Sis were setting the table for dinner, Leigh asked her mom, "Do you remember the nurse you were talking to in Granddaddy Thurman's room?"

"Which one."

"The one who said she'd try our church."

Aunt Helen stopped what she was doing at the sink to look at Leigh. "Emma Hammond, if my memory serves me. Why?"

"Just curious," Leigh said, shrugging off the question.

Squinting at Leigh, Aunt Helen asked her, "Should I be worried?"

After saying, "No, ma'am." Leigh said, "Come on, y'all," to us kids then headed for the playroom.

Aunt Helen told us not to leave the house so close to dinnertime. She turned her back to us then turned on a power mixer, a sign we might get something good for desert. On the way Leigh snuck the phonebook out of the livingroom under her shirt.

In the playroom she handed Sis a pencil and paper and told her to look up the phone number for the Glocks. She told Tripp to go spy on their mom. "If she's gonna use the other phone, you gotta warn me before she picks up or she'll hear me."

Sis read the Glock's phone number to Leigh. Leigh dialed it. Moments later she said, "Can I speak to "Sandy" then after a pause, "Hey, Sandy, do you know a kid named Hammond?"

After another pause Leigh asked her if his mother was a nurse at the hospital and what his first name was.

Leigh put her hand over the mouth piece, told Sis, "His name is Rory and he lives on Southeast 2nd Street."

For some reason that upset Sis. I knew it did because she stared out into space. Mom did that when she was upset. Like the people in the movie "Invasion of the Body Snatchers."

Leigh put her hand over the mouthpiece. "Psst, Sarah."

"Huh?"

"Write down Southeast 2nd Street."

Before hanging up Leigh said to her friend, "I was just wondering." Then she sent Mattie to get Tripp and told Sis to look up the address for the Hammonds.

"The only listing for a Hammond on Southeast 2nd Street is for is Virgil Hammond at number 243. That must be his Dad."

Tripp asked Leigh if she was really going there.

"Yeah, and you're all invited."

Sis surprised me by asking Leigh when we were going, but then I remembered Rory, and knew why she wanted to go.

Mattie asked Sis. "Does that mean you're going with us, Aunt Sarah?"

Sis smiled and told her, "Yes, but I'm not your aunt."

Mattie jumped up and down and clapped her hands and said, "Oh goodie."

Leigh told her to hush.

After that Tripp and Leigh and I played pool. Sis said she didn't want to. Mattie, who did want to, but was too short, called us meanies.

Sis was looking through the sheet music in the piano bench when Mattie went over to her and tugged on her shirtsleeve. "Will you play *Chutes and Ladders* with me, Aunt Sarah?"

Sis frowned.

Mattie's chin scrunched up, as though she was about to cry. "You don't you like me, do you?"

"Of course I do, Mattie."

Mattie smiled ear to ear. "Then you will play *Chutes and Ladders* with me?"

Leigh snickered. Mattie gave her a dirty look. Sis said she

didn't know how.

Talking through a big cheery smile, Mattie said, "Don't worry, Aunt Sarah, I'll teach you."

Sis looked at me first then at Leigh. I think she wanted someone to rescue her. As far as I was concerned she was on her own. While she sat there looking confused, and sort of dumb, if you want to know the truth, Mattie took the game off the shelf and set it up on their folding card table. Slump-shouldered and defeated looking, Sis pulled a chair up to the table. Mattie told her to spin for a number. Sis spun a five.

Mattie spun a two then told Sis to go first.

"What do I do?"

"Pick one of those little people thingies to move then spin again."

After spinning a four, Sis counted out the spaces, stopping on one at the bottom of a ladder.

"If you stop on a space with a ladder you climb it," Mattie said, tapping the board with a tiny index finger. "And if you stop at the top of a chute you have to slide down."

"I didn't know that."

"That's why it's called *Chutes and Ladders*, silly."

Sis blushed, said she had to do something then left. After throwing her arms up in an exaggerated show of frustration, Mattie took Sis' turn then went on to play the game by herself.

"YOU'LL BE SORRY"

Then it was Sunday, another church day, and that always made me antsy. This time Sis and I were the first ones out front. I tried throwing a driveway stone over the pine trees along the pasture fence, an impossibly long throw.

Sis asked me why I always went along with Leigh's crazy schemes.

I shrugged my shoulders. Sis would call me stupid if she knew why.

"You're afraid she'll think you're a coward, aren't you?"

I turned my back on her and threw a stone so hard my arm hurt afterward. She told me I shouldn't care what other people think. I was glad she hadn't figured out that it was Margo I was worried about. I threw another stone as hard as I could, sore arm and all. It sailed through a tree barely half way up the trunk. I turned around to make a face at Sis but Aunt Helen had come out so I didn't.

We didn't all fit in Uncle Bud's shiny blue Pontiac Bonneville, at least not so it was comfortable. Sis sat up front between Uncle Bud and Aunt Helen. The rest of us kids sat in the back, all four of us. Leigh and I got the window seats. Poor Tripp sat in the middle, but Leigh had it worse, because Mattie sat on her lap. I liked taking two cars better, even if it meant riding with Mom.

I deserved extra credit for being in church that day because it lasted forever. After church we went to Grandmother

Thurman's house. Aunt Helen told us to play outside and behave ourselves. Leigh begged money from her to buy popsicles at the corner store. Aunt Helen grimaced but gave her a handful of change.

After Aunt Helen went inside, Tripp said to Leigh, "That's not enough for bus fare."

"I know that, silly. We'll use the money we collected for Amu's bail to pay for the bus."

"Then why'd you ask for money?"

"Boy are you thick."

"Oh yeah, then tell me why, Miss Ever-so-clever?"

"If Mom noticed we were gone she'd look for us. Then we'd be in a heap of trouble. This way she'll think we're hanging out near the store eating candy."

"But won't she start to wonder if we're gone a long time?"

After calling Tripp a worry wart, Leigh headed for the store. From Grandmother's we walked two blocks to the bus stop. When the bus came Leigh asked the driver if his bus went to Southeast 2nd Street. The nice man promised to tell us when we got there.

Tripp and I got into a heated discussion about how Superman got from his home planet, Krypton, to Earth, and why he came here. From where the bus dropped us off we walked two blocks to a house so dumpy-looking I wouldn't have knocked on the door for all the tea in China. Of course it didn't stop Leigh from knocking on it.

Scruffy's kid, Rory, opened the door a crack. He was wearing a not-so-white white tee shirt with half a dozen grease smudges on it. I scooched over behind Tripp so Rory wouldn't see me. You'd have thought we were truant officers the way he looked at us. That is, until he saw my sister. He smiled at her. She blushed mightily. No question about it. My sister had a crush on the guy, which was too weird to even think about, especially if she was right and Rory's dad was a killer. Figures that would be my sister's first crush.

Leigh asked him, "You Rory?"

"What if I am?"

Leigh shoved the door open and pushed her way past him, with him saying, "What the hell?"

You'd have thought Mattie was Leigh's shadow the way she slipped in behind her,

Rory told us we couldn't be there, but didn't step forward to back up the threat.

When I walked past him, Rory, who looked surprised to see me, whispered, "Hey, you're that Yankee punk from the hospital, aren't ya?"

Tripp and Sis came in after me. I don't think they heard what Rory said to me. Leigh told him we had some questions for him.

"Yeah? What about?"

"Sheriff Ritchey."

"I already talked to him about the robbery."

Tripp and Leigh both looked surprised when he said that, as though someone had poked them somewhere naughty. But not Sis. She frowned. I think she'd figured out something she didn't like.

Rory did a double take when he saw our reactions. "You didn't come here to ask me about the robbery, did you?"

When none of us said anything, Rory squinted at us as though we'd gone out of focus. "What the hell is this?"

Stepping in front of Leigh, fearless little Mattie pointed a tiny finger at Rory and told him, "Give me back my uncle's dragon."

"Huh?"

Mattie stomped her foot. "My uncle's dragon. Give it back"

Leigh told her to shush. Then tipping her head a little to the side Leigh asked Rory, "You don't know, do you?"

"Know what?"

"He's dead."

"Who's dead?"

When Leigh said, "Sheriff Ritchey," Rory blinked. His head

jerked back and he opened his mouth to say something but didn't. Instead he stood there looking even dumber than usual, so I was pretty sure it was news to him.

Leigh said to Sis, "I could use some help here, Sarah. We probably won't get another chance to ask him questions."

Even though she was obviously upset, she stepped forward, and this time she wasn't all smiles and blushing when she asked Rory, "When did you talk to Sheriff Ritchey?"

"What difference does it make?"

"Was it Tuesday night?"

"What if it was?"

"That's the night Sheriff Ritchey was killed."

Rory looked like a kid who'd eaten a piece of meat loaded with gristle and couldn't spit it out because he was a guest at someone's house and his parents were there. "I don't know anything about that."

Then Sis caught him off guard, like at the end of every Perry Mason show when he catches the murderer in a lie. "That night your mom asked Mrs. Thurman when she'd be going home. She did that so you'd know when it was safe to rob Grandma's house."

Sis was getting to be a regular Sherlock Holmes.

Rory scowled at her. "I don't see what all the fuss is about. It was just some crappy old jewelry."

Sis went quiet for a moment after that, rethinking her opinion of Rory, I guess. Her last words to him were a warning. "Sheriff Ritchey didn't arrest you because you're a minor, but when the police find out what your mom did they'll arrest her as an accomplice to the robbery."

That put an end to Rory's tough guy act. "It was my dad's idea. Mom tried to talk him out of it."

"Did you tell Sheriff Ritchey that the robbery was your dad's idea?"

"You need to leave, now."

"If you did tell him that, he would've tried to arrest your dad."

"You're gonna regret it if you're here when he gets home."

Leaving sounded like a pretty good idea to me, especially when Rory puffed out his chest and balled up his fists like a bully looking for trouble.

Leave it to Leigh to come right out and say something that could start trouble. "Did your dad kill Sheriff Ritchey?"

Rory yelled at us to get out. Sis, whose face had been just inches from his, cringed and backed up then turned around and left in a hurry. Tripp grabbed Mattie's hand and followed her. I was close behind them. Leigh was the last one to leave.

Rory yelled at us from the doorway. "I'm telling my dad what you said."

THE CASTLE

By the time I got outside Sis was half way to the road and walking fast. I yelled to her to wait up. She stopped and turned around and asked me what I wanted.

She looked so mad I almost told her to forget it, almost. "I saw you and Rory talking at the hospital."

"So what?"

"Leigh thinks you like him?"

After saying, "I don't want to talk about it," Sis turned around.

I said, "So you do like him," to her as she walked away.

She stopped and spun back around to glare at me. "What'd I just tell you?"

"Your boyfriend Rory is a real creep."

"He acts badly because he doesn't feel comfortable around you, the same way you felt uncomfortable around Amu when we first met him."

"That's different."

"No it's not."

I gave up and walked away. I wasn't anything like Rory. I didn't try to pick a fight with Amu, and I didn't pull a knife on him. If she liked the murderer's son who robbed her Grandmother, there wasn't much point in arguing with her.

I waited for Tripp and Mattie to catch up and walked with them. Sis had walked on ahead to wait for us at the bus stop. When we got there she told us we were in danger. After looking around nervously Tripp asked her why.

"Not in front of Mattie."

"Why not in front of me?"

Leigh pointed at a Chevy Impala parked down the street and told Mattie, "Go stand by that red car and wait for us."

Mattie crossed her arms and stuck her tongue out then stepped back, so when Leigh reached for her, Mattie safely dodged her hand.

After calling Leigh a, "Poopy stink-face," Mattie skipped off toward the red car.

Leigh shook her head then asked Sis what all the fuss was about.

"There's no telling what Rory's dad will do when Rory tells him we think he killed your uncle."

Tripp moaned, asked Sis, "Do you think he'd kill Mattie, or one of us?"

Sis shrugged her shoulders.

Leigh said, "Y'all are crazy."

Mattie yelled. "Can I come back now?"

Leigh waved to her to come back. We caught the bus a few minutes later. With the afternoon sun pouring in through the windows sideways, the ride was so hot that lying under a shade tree when we got back to Grandmother Thurman's felt good.

I should've worried more about Rory and his dad, but I had that wonderful, "the lazy summer days will last forever" feeling. With no chores and no homework to waste my precious time on, school might as well have been a thousand years away.

After a while Leigh pointed up at the sky. "Hey y'all, check out that cloud, it looks like an angel."

I asked her where. She leaned toward me so I could sight down her arm as she pointed at a cloud shaped more like a bird than an angel.

Pointing at a clump of puffy clouds near the horizon, Mattie declared proudly, "I see a fairy castle."

Leigh said she didn't see it. I didn't see it either, but the line between real and make-believe is a lot fuzzier for kids Mattie's age.

Poor Mattie, Leigh wouldn't let it go. "I think you're making it up just like you did the dragon."

"Am not," Mattie said, her voice cracking a little as she stabbed the sky with a tiny index finger. "It's right there."

"Yeah, sure," Leigh said, "you can see a castle that no one else can."

With her lower lip quivering, Mattie blinked several times. Then my sister of all people said she saw it.

"See," Mattie said between sniffles.

Try as I might I still didn't see anything that looked even the teeniest bit like a castle. Leigh told Mattie that Sis was just being nice.

Mattie called her a, "Stupid poopy-pants."

That's when Aunt Helen came out to tell us we were leaving. For the ride back to my cousins' house Mattie sat on Tripp's lap. About halfway there Aunt Helen twisted around in her seat to look at us. "Y'all sure are quiet."

Mattie told her, "That's because Leigh's a big a meanie poop."

"Leigh?"

"What?"

"Were you mean to your sister?"

"No, ma'am."

"Were too," Mattie said.

Aunt Helen shook her head. "I should've known better than to ask."

Back at my cousins, we played croquet until we were called in for dinner. Somewhere in the middle of the second game I began to feel as though something was wrong, and not because I was losing, which I was. And I couldn't blame the weather, which wasn't especially hot or muggy for a change.

I was using my mallet to line up my next shot when I noticed that my ball was in the shade. That's when I realized I'd been expecting Aunt Helen to call us in for dinner. The shadows were longer than they should be. I'd been ignoring the passing of summer because it meant the start of school getting closer, its dark shadow looming just over my horizon, threatening my endless summer freedom.

School would start soon and last for a whole nine months, which is almost forever. My only freedom other than Saturdays would be Sunday afternoons and a few minutes before dinner on school days. When my free time becomes precious I have trouble deciding what to do. And even if I do think of something, it's hard to enjoy it knowing I don't have much time.

DANA

The next morning after my cousins had finished their chores we argued over how to split up into two teams for kickball so it would be a fair game. We were still arguing when Aunt Helen came to the back door.

Holding it open, she told us she was going to the barn to look for Uncle Bud and told us to go wait for her in the car. Leigh asked her why she didn't just wait until he came home for lunch.

"Because your father's been negotiating a cattle deal. The buyer just called to say he'd take a hundred head. I need to find your father before the man changes his mind. And y'all are coming with me so I don't have to worry about you getting into trouble."

Aunt Helen let Sis stay at their house to practice the piano, but wouldn't hear of Sis babysitting us after what had happened the last time. So we piled into the car without Sis. Leigh sat up front with her mom, which left Tripp and me in the back with Mattie sitting between us. When Tripp and I started playing Rock Paper Scissors Mattie said she wanted to play. Tripp told her "no."

"Momma, they won't let me play."

"Let your sister play, Tripp."

"But Rock, Paper, Scissors is for only two people."

By then Aunt Helen had stopped at the first pasture gate. "Forget the game and go open the gate."

Tripp got out and shuffled toward the gate. Aunt Helen

151

rolled her window down and leaned out. "Come on, Tripp, I don't have all day."

The moment he had the gate open Aunt Helen drove through, leaving him standing there watching us drive away without him.

Leigh looked back at Tripp and laughed. "Hey, you forgot Tripp."

"We'll pick him up on the way back."

I looked back. Tripp shook his head then kicked at the dirt. Then he started walking after us.

Uncle Bud was standing in a clump of steers. Dana was running around them barking up a storm. Every now and then one of them would raise its head to look at Dana like a curiosity then go back to its feed. Aunt Helen honked the horn. Uncle Bud waved to us.

Dana saw us then and trotted toward us wagging his tail. Mattie stepped on my foot as she pushed her way over to my window then stood in the wheel well. Dana stood on his hind legs with his front paws on the car. Mattie stuck her face out the window. You'd have thought it was covered in dog treats the way Dana slobbered all over it.

Leigh made a face, said, "Ew, Momma, look what Mattie's doing."

"Mattie, don't let him do that."

Mattie ignored her mother. So did Dana.

Uncle Bud had come over to the car. He was so tall that standing next to Aunt Helen's window I could only see him from the waist down. He asked her why she was there.

"That buyer fella called, said he'd take a hundred head, more if you've got 'em. He wants you to call him."

Uncle Bud told her that one of the calves was due for its medicine. "It won't take but five minutes. Then you can give me a ride back to the house."

Aunt Helen told us we didn't have to wait, that we could walk back to the house. Leigh was out the door in a flash and running across the pasture toward the road. I ran after her.

When we reached the fence along the road I looked back. Tripp had made it to the car and was bringing Mattie. They were half a pasture behind us. Dana wasn't going to miss a chance to be with Mattie. He was running along the fence looking for a place to crawl under.

Leigh yelled, "Race you to our mailbox."

I really poured it on, running so fast I felt a breeze on my face. By surprising me with the race Leigh had taken an early ten foot lead, but I was gaining on her. I did pass her, but not how I'd expected. She looked back then stopped so hard her feet made slapping sounds on the pavement. I stopped to see why she stopped.

Tripp and Mattie had made it to the road and were taking their sweet time, Tripp loping along in the grass beside the road, Dana trotting in the road, weaving back and forth alongside Mattie, who was between them on the edge of the pavement looking down at her legs, running with her knees together and her feet splayed out, like a cartoon character. They weren't facing traffic so they didn't know that a car was bearing down on them, and fast.

Waving her arms, Leigh pointed at the car and yelled, "Look out. Behind you."

Tripp stopped and turned around. The car was nearly on top of them. I expected it to swerve. It didn't. I expected to hear tires squealing. I didn't.

Leigh yelled, "Look out, Mattie."

I felt helpless. Tripp yanked Mattie's arm, hard. She sprawled into the ditch. The engine roared. Dana looked back. I looked away. Dana squealed. I watched the car speed past me. There was no mistaking the stupid-looking hood scoop. When I turned around Dana lay in the road.

Leigh yelled to Tripp, "Get Mattie away from there."

I heard car doors in the distance, saw Uncle Bud's car headed for the road kicking up a cloud of dust. When he got to Dana he parked across the road to block traffic.

When Aunt Helen got out of the car, she said, "Oh Lawdy."

Uncle Bud picked up Mattie and put her in the back seat of the car. He told Aunt Helen to take her home then bring the car back so he could take Dana to Doc Russel's. He told Tripp, "Go with them and stay with Mattie."

There was blood in the road next to Dana. Leigh was kneeling over him crying, the only time I ever saw her cry. Aunt Helen came back alone a few minutes later with a blanket spread out on the back seat. Uncle Bud and Leigh put Dana in the car then Uncle Bud took him to the vet's.

Aunt Helen and Leigh and I walked to their house. On the way, Leigh told her mom, "That car never even slowed down."

"There's all kinds of bad people in the world, Leigh. I wish there weren't. But that's the way of it."

"But why does the Lord allow it, Momma?"

Aunt Helen shook her head. "I don't rightly know, child, but God must have a purpose for it."

I wanted to tell them I knew who's car it was but wasn't comfortable doing that with all of them upset and talking God stuff.

Sis was sitting on the front steps waiting for us. She told Leigh she was sorry. I told Leigh she had blood on her shirtsleeve. She just shrugged her shoulders.

All of us ended up in the dining room. Mattie asked her mom why God let it happen.

"Bad things are just as much a part of God's plan as good things."

"Then it's a stupid plan."

"We don't speak ill of the Lord in this house, young lady."

Mattie frowned.

Aunt Helen patted her lap, said to Mattie, "Come here and sit with me."

Chin up in the air, looking at her mom defiantly, Mattie said, "God's plan is a poopy. And if you don't think so, you're poopy too." Then she jumped off of Helen's lap and ran out of the room.

Aunt Helen told us to leave Mattie alone, and that she just

needed a good cry. An hour or more later we heard the car pull into the carport. Uncle Bud wasn't half way through the kitchen door when Tripp asked him if Dana was okay. He turned a dining chair away from the table, slumping forward a little when he sat down, as though he'd had a hard day. Mattie came back, eyes red from crying. Uncle Bud swept her up onto his lap. She asked him when Dana would be coming home.

He looked older than I'd ever seen him. "I don't know, princess. He's in pretty bad shape."

Mattie tugged on the necklace Amu had given her until the string broke and the stuff Amu had threaded on it sprayed all over the room. She threw the string on the floor then, putting her arms around Uncle Bud's neck, tucked her head against his shoulder and sobbed. A few moments later her head popped up. Her tears had left a wet spot on his shirt. She asked her dad to take her to see Dana.

"He wouldn't know you, Princess. We'll go see him when he's feeling better."

Mattie snuggled back against her dad's shoulder. I followed Tripp's example and crawled around on the floor picking up pieces of the necklace. Then we went outside and sat on the front steps with Sis and Leigh.

Sitting on the top step hunched over her knees with her arms around her legs, Sis was folded up like a dead bug. "Taking Dana to the vet must have been hard on your dad."

Luckily, Sis didn't say anything more about that. It wasn't the best time for Sis to tell them how tough it was on their dad, especially with his brother dead. And speaking of telling people things, maybe it wasn't the best time to tell my cousins what I'd seen, but I couldn't keep quiet about it any longer.

"KILLER OR NO, I'M GOING"

I told them that it was Scruffy's car that hit Dana.

Leigh asked me how I knew.

"I saw him leaning on that same car in the parking lot at the hospital."

Sis asked me if I was sure.

"Jeez, you never believe me."

"How do you know it's the same car? Maybe it just looks the same."

"Because there can't be more than one vomit-green Ford Falcon with a big, dumb-looking red hood scoop."

"Oh dear," Sis said, her shoulders drooping visibly.

Leigh asked her what was wrong.

"I bet it was a warning."

"You think so?"

Mattie came out to join us then. "What was what?" she asked.

When Leigh told her, "Never you mind," poor Mattie looked as though Leigh had broken her favorite doll.

That night instead of thinking about Dana, or Margo, or a leaky boat and alligators, I wondered what the rest of my summer would be like, wondered if I'd get to go fishing with Grandpa Dawson, or go to Keystone Beach for a picnic at

156

the ocean, or maybe even go to see the alligator farm in St. Augustine.

The next morning my cousins badgered Aunt Helen until she agreed to make burgers for breakfast, something my mother would never, ever do.

Mattie begged Aunt Helen to make hot Dr. Pepper for us. "Please, Momma."

"Oh, Mattie, Sarah and Lainard will think we're plumb crazy," but a few whiney "pleases" later Aunt Helen gave in. I figured she was being nice to my cousins because of what happened to Dana and their uncle.

She had us each come get a plate and a burger bun. The sound and smell of burgers sizzling in the frying pan made my mouth water and my stomach grumble until Aunt Helen put a plate of them on the table. You'd have thought Mattie was playing slap jack the way her hand shot out and grabbed one to put on her bun. Aunt Helen scolded her for using her fingers. Mattie reached for the Ketchup. Aunt Helen told Tripp' to help her with it. He squirted a swirl of it on her burger. She told him it was an ugly swirl then demanded more. He made another swirl.

"More."

Tripp told her she had enough. Mattie stuck her tongue out at him.

Aunt Helen gave each of us a mug of warm Dr. Pepper. I liked it so much I wondered why they didn't advertise drinking it that way. The wall phone rang about halfway through my burger. Aunt Helen told Leigh to get it.

Leigh answered it then held it out for her dad. "It's Doc Russell."

Uncle Bud wasn't on the phone long and didn't say much besides, "Hello Doc.," and, "If you think that's best," and, "thanks for calling."

I thought the meaning was pretty obvious, but Mattie didn't get it until she saw the look on her dad's face when he turned around. You can bet she started crying then, standing up so fast she knocked her chair over as she ran for the door to the

157

hallway. Aunt Helen rushed after her.

Tears welled up in Leigh's eyes. "Did you have to, Daddy?"

Uncle Bud let out a long, slow, sigh before answering. "Doc said Dana was suffering."

"But..."

"Kids, Mattie was Dana's favorite. So this will be especially hard on her."

Sis elbowed me. "Come on Leonard, we should go outside."

I followed her out and sat on the back steps with her. She folded up like a dead bug again. Sis and I had always had pets growing up. I didn't remember any of them dying. I asked her about that. She said she didn't want to talk about it. That was it for talk until Tripp and Leigh came out. They sat on the bottom step with their backs to us.

Sis said, "I'm sorry about Dana."

I said, "Me too."

Leigh, who was staring off into space, said, "It's my fault."

Sis told her it wasn't her fault, but I think that just made her feel worse because she choked out, "Dana would still be alive if we hadn't gone to see Rory."

Tripp asked Leigh what we should do.

"Nothing."

"We gotta do something."

Slumped over, looking down at her feet, Leigh said, "The last thing I did got Dana killed."

Sis announced that she was going in to practice. I almost envied her having something to do; almost. I asked Leigh and Tripp if they wanted to do something. Tripp said no. Leigh didn't answer. I went inside and searched the playroom until I found some cards. The six of spades was missing from the deck. I played solitaire with them anyway.

I soon went back outside. Not because of the missing six of spades. I couldn't stand listening to Sis play the same thing a hundred times. A teary-eyed Mattie came outside a short while later. She sat down close to me, close enough that the others wouldn't have heard her whisper, "Leonard?"

"Yeah?"

"Do dogs go to heaven when they die?"

The idea of answering a religious question scared the bejesus out of me. I wanted to help poor Mattie but was too afraid of telling her something wrong. "I'm sorry, Mattie, but you should ask your Mom about that."

Her mouth turned down and her eyes watered. Then, bent over like a partially deflated doll, she walked away to sit by herself. When Sis came out Mattie sat next to her and asked her the same question.

"He's one of God's creatures."

"So he's in heaven?"

"What did they teach you in Sunday school?"

"They didn't teach us about dogs."

I guess Sis got scared then too because she told Mattie to ask her dad. Mattie went straight to the kitchen door and called for her dad.

"He stepped outside a moment later. "Yes, Princess?"

"Dana's one of God's creatures. Aunt Sarah said so."

He seemed to think about it then nodded his head.

"So I'll get to pet him when I die?"

Uncle Bud told her they'd talk about that another time.

Mattie frowned and stomped her foot then turned around and bounded down the steps. Uncle Bud went back inside. Mattie walked out to the fence and sat in the grass facing away from us. Nobody said anything after that until Sis asked Tripp what he did with Mattie's necklace. He fished a handful of necklace pieces and string out of his pocket and gave it to her. And that was it for talk until Aunt Helen called Leigh in to help her make lunch. Sis said she'd help too and went inside.

A little while later Aunt Helen called Tripp and Mattie and me in for lunch. She and Uncle Bud had egg salad sandwiches. Us kids had PBJs. During lunch Sis put Mattie's necklace on the table in front of her. It looked as good as new. Mattie frowned at it.

"Don't you want it?" Sis asked.

"If it was real magic, Dana would still be here."

159

"The magic wasn't meant for Dana. It was meant for you."

"Magic schmagic."

Leigh said, "Jeez, what a grouch."

Then with a devilish little grin Mattie announced, "Leigh's got something to tell you, Momma."

Aunt Helen put her sandwich down. "Leigh?"

Leigh grinned at Mattie before asking Aunt Helen, "You know that nurse, Mrs. Hammond?"

"What about her?"

"Her husband killed Uncle Pete."

"Where on earth did you get such a cockamamie idea?"

"Go on, Mattie, tell her."

That explained Leigh's grin – if she got in trouble Mattie would too.

"He has Uncle Pete's dragon."

"If this is some kind of joke, it's not funny. That Mrs. Hammond is a hardworking, God-fearing Christian and doesn't deserve to be slandered. Now I don't want to hear any more about it."

Mattie asked her mom what slandered meant. Aunt Helen told us to go outside, which meant no dessert, one of the worst things that could happen, next to getting spanked.

We met out by the bridge, all of us except Sis.

Leigh asked me why she didn't come out.

"She's practicing her piano junk."

"Well I warned her, didn't I?"

"Huh?"

"If Momma decides someone's a good Christian, there's no telling her any different."

Tripp asked Leigh, "Now what do we do?"

"Go see Rory's Dad."

"What if he's the killer?"

"Y'all don't have to go with me if you're scared."

Mattie announced that she was going. Leigh told her she wasn't. Mattie pouted.

Leigh turned to me, "What about you, Leonard? You want

160

to go with me?"

I nodded my head then got a stomach full of butterflies.

"Tripp?"

He groaned.

Mattie picked a dandelion, put her thumb under the flower and tried to flick it at Leigh. It fell in the grass by Mattie's feet. Leigh picked one and flicked it at Mattie. It hit Mattie on the forehead.

Mattie yelled, "Stupid poopy-face."

Tripp picked one and held it up to show Mattie how you do it. She tried again. It fell in the grass again. She stomped her foot. After that we played hide-and-seek until it was time to go in.

That night while I was waiting for sleep to claim me, I remembered Dana and the way he squealed when he was hit. It got me thinking about my dog and how bad I'd feel if she died. It helped me understand how Mattie felt about Dana, but only sort of, because the whole dying thing had never made much sense to me.

And poor Mattie had lost her uncle too. The last time I'd seen him was the summer before when he had a pig roast at his house. I think there was about a million people there that day. About the same height as Uncle Bud, but heavier, with a big toothy smile, he reminded me of Roy Rodger's sidekick, Jingles, only not as goofy.

I figured Tripp was still awake because he wasn't snoring. "Hey, Tripp?"

"Yeah?"

"Do you ever think about where we go when we die?"

"We go to heaven."

"How do you know?"

"The bible says so."

"But what if the people who wrote it were wrong?"

"Don't let Momma hear you say that."

I flipped my pillow over so it would feel cooler. It did for about a second, which was how long it took for Margo to pop into my thoughts. I pretended we were sitting in rockers on Grandpa

Dawsons' porch and I had just said something she thought was very smart, and this time Tommy Lee wasn't there to spoil things. Next thing I knew Mattie was shaking my toes to wake me for breakfast.

"WE SHOULD FINISH WHAT WE STARTED"

After breakfast, all five of us were out back lazing in the grass trying to think of something to do when Leigh spotted a frog out near the fence. "Hey Mattie, there goes your prince."

"Ooh," Mattie said, "catch him for me Tripp."

Trip grinned at Mattie before going after the frog. Catching it easily and bringing it back to her.

"Mattie," Leigh said, threateningly, "don't you dare."

Leigh of all people should've known you never say that to Mattie, and as if to prove it, Mattie raised the frog to her lips and kissed it.

Tripp laughed. Leigh made a face like she'd stepped in fresh dog poop. I couldn't do anything but watch. Poor Mattie didn't know that frog's pee when you frighten them, which it did, on her dress. Mattie laughed then put the frog down.

Leigh told her to go in and get some clean clothes, which she did. I wondered how she was going to explain that to Aunt Helen. She came out a few minutes later wearing a dress that was really puffy from the waist down. If she pushed it in in one place it would puff out somewhere else, something she did repeatedly while giggling to herself. She laughed hysterically when she noticed us laughing about it.

When we lost interest in Mattie's antics, Tripp asked

163

Leigh, "What're you going to do about Rory's dad?"

Leigh shrugged her shoulders. It was more of a droopy "I give up" shrug than an "I don't know" shrug. My mother would've called it moping, and if it was me, she would've said, "If you don't stop that right now I'll give you something to mope about."

Tripp told her that feeling sorry for herself wouldn't bring her uncle back, or Dana either.

Leigh tipped her head and frowned at him as though he'd said something she didn't understand. "Wow, Tripp, that was really weird."

"What was?"

"What you said. It sounded like something Daddy would say."

"Well I think we should finish what we started."

I asked him what we should do. He asked Sis what we should do.

"Get Rory's dad to admit that he killed your uncle."

I asked her how.

"If we accuse him of doing it, he might get mad and admit to it without thinking."

"He'd have to be pretty stupid to do that in front of five kids, wouldn't he?"

"It might work if just one of us confronted him?"

"Wouldn't that be dangerous?"

"Definitely."

"Who'd be crazy enough to do that?"

We all looked at Leigh. She nodded her head. I told her it would be her word against a grownup's. She asked if any of us had a better idea. We all shook our heads. Tripp asked her if she was going back to Rory's house.

"Yeah."

He called her crazy. She called him a pansy.

"What if he's not home?"

"I'll go call right now and find out." And with that she headed for the house.

To keep Mattie happy while we waited for Leigh, Tripp helped her do headstands. If he held her by her ankles she could hold one for almost a second before folding up like an old road map. Tripp made it look easy. Sis refused to try. I could do one without help, but not nearly as long as Tripp could.

When Leigh came back out we all gathered around her, all of us except Mattie who snuck up behind Sis and yelled, "Tag you're it" then ran away.

Leigh called Mattie back, told her she had a job for her. "But you've gotta promise not to tell anyone."

"Not even Momma?"

"Especially Momma."

Mattie took a long time to think it over before agreeing. Leigh told her she had to promise. Mattie nodded her head.

"Cross your heart and hope to spit?"

Mattie drew a giant imaginary "X" on her chest with her index finger then pretended to spit, making a dry "pteu" sound.

"I guess that'll have to do. Now run inside and get my notebook. It's in the playroom on the pool table.

"Why?"

"Because."

"Because why?"

"Because I don't want Momma to find it."

"How come?"

"It's got Rory's name and address in it."

"So?"

"So if Momma sees it she'll get suspicious."

"Why can't Tripp do it?"

"Because Momma won't suspect you." But it took Leigh saying the magic words, "I guess you don't want to go with us next time," to get Mattie running for the house, stiff little arms swinging wildly, big floppy rubber boots slapping her shins.

When Mattie was out of earshot Leigh said, "We don't have much time before she comes back, so listen up. The county fair opens today. Rory said his dad got a job there setting up tents, and that he'd probably be there until late. And I bet he's gonna be there late because the beer tent stays open really late."

"Wow, Leigh," Sis said, "I can't believe Rory told you that."

Leigh grinned at her. "I told him I was a nurse and that I needed to talk to his dad about the results of his blood test."

"So you're gonna talk to him today?" Tripp asked.

"Yep."

"Oh yeah? How are you gonna do that?"

"I'll go to the fair."

"How are you gonna do that?"

"It opens at noon. I'll go after lunch."

"How are you gonna get there?"

"I'll take the farm truck."

"That old thing. It'll never make it."

"Jeez, lighten up, will ya, Tripp?"

"There'll be police at the fair," Sis said, "and you don't look old enough to drive."

Leigh eyed Sis, "But you do."

I couldn't help snickering at the thought of Sis driving their old stick shift farm truck. Sure enough, Sis told Leigh she couldn't possibly do that.

Leigh said she'd get Amu to drive then asked if any of us wanted to go with her. It was a stupid idea, and I really didn't want to go but said I would because of Margo.

Tripp said he wouldn't, "Not for a million dollars."

Leigh told him, "Fine, then you're staying here with Mattie."

"If you don't take her with you she'll tell Momma. You know she will."

"Don't let her."

"How can I stop her? You know what she's like."

"Suit yourself. But if she rats on me you'll be sorry."

Leigh asked Sis if she was coming. Sis shook her head no.

"What if I said Please?"

"The answer's still no."

"Then I guess it's just Leonard and me."

THE COUNTY FAIR

Out back near the bridge, after lunch, Leigh said to Mattie, "Why don't you and Tripp have a tea party? Wouldn't that be fun?"

Tripp told Leigh, "Forget it. I'm not having a dang tea party."

Mattie eyed her sister with suspicion. "You're going somewhere aren't you, Leigh?"

Leigh got up close in Tripp's face. "You'd better think of something, 'cause if I get in trouble it's your fault."

"How's it my fault?"

Mattie announced that she was going. Leigh told her she wasn't.

"Fine, then I'm telling Momma."

For a moment or two Leigh seemed to think about something. I thought she might give up on going, but then she pulled her sleeve up to show us a blackish-purple bruise on her arm. "Tripp, if you don't come with us to keep an eye on Mattie, I'll tell Momma that's where you hit me."

"Hey, no fair. Mattie did that when we were playing leap frog."

"Who's Momma gonna believe?"

He groaned and rolled his eyes and shook his head, but I knew he was coming with us.

Sis knelt in the grass in front of Mattie. She took out the necklace Amu had given Mattie, and told her to hold still.

"I don't want it."

"Then wear it for me."

"Only if you come with us."

Sis let out a defeated-sounding sigh, which meant she was coming with us. Nice work Mattie.

Mattie turned around so Sis could tie the necklace around her neck then said. "But it's still piggy poop."

"Come on y'all," Leigh said, "we've gotta hurry." Then she headed for the barn. Mattie led Sis by the hand. Tripp and I brought up the rear. Uncle Bud's old farm pickup was parked next to the barn. Leigh told us his dad always left the keys in it because, "No one would be dumb enough to steal an old junk heap like that." Leigh told Sis she could ride up front. She told the rest of us, "Y'all can get in the back."

Tripp mumbled something then dropped the tailgate and hopped in. I helped Mattie up then climbed in. The three of us sat with our backs against the cab.

Before driving away Leigh, leaned out the driver's window to tell us, "Y'all had better hold on, 'cause it's gonna get bumpy," and she wasn't kidding.

When we got near the cabin, Amu came out to greet us. I bet he'd heard my poor butt pounding the truck bed. He asked Leigh what we were doing there.

"The guy who killed Sheriff Ritchey is at the county fair. We're going there to find him."

Shaking his head, Amu told her, "You shouldn't do that."

"We're going," Leigh said, slipping the clutch, "with or without you."

The truck lurched forward. Amu watched us leave. I couldn't help thinking that he was right, that we were making a mistake. We bumped and bounced our way through a series of pastures to the Williston Cutoff then took backroads all the way to the fairgrounds to avoid the police. Leigh parked in a field full of cars near the entrance, and judging by the number of cars I saw, there must have been a million people at the Alachua County Fair that day.

Sis was slow getting out of the truck and slow to join us and she did not look happy. Leigh asked her what was wrong.

"What happens when we confront Virgil?"

"We tell him we know what he did."

"It's too dangerous, Leigh, especially without Amu?"

After saying, "Fine, I'll go by myself," Leigh headed for the gate to the fairway. Mattie hurried after her, running to keep up. Tripp followed them. I could join them to look for a killer or wait at the truck and look like a chicken. Sis hesitated. I asked her if she was going with Leigh.

She turned the question back at me. "Are you?"

"I asked you first."

She made a face at me then headed for the fairway. As loud as the noises from the fair had been in the parking lot, they were deafening on the midway, a crowded path of trampled field grass lined with food stands and games and rides. As we hurried passed them, the carnies running the games yelled challenges to us. The smells coming from the food stands presented their own challenges, daring us to pass them by without eating any of the delicious-smelling fried foods, until we got more than a few feet away and the aromas mixed with carny-worker body stink and the diesel exhaust of the ride machinery. Add to that the occasional whiff of a pipe or cigar.

We let Tripp and Mattie walk in front of us so we wouldn't lose track of them, a good idea that didn't work out because Mattie stopped every five feet to point out something. The next time she stopped she squealed, "Ooh, look, they have candy clouds. I want some."

Leigh told her we didn't have time.

"Please, can we? I promise I won't ask for anything else."

"Yeah, okay, if it'll shut you up. But remember that you promised not to ask for anything else."

We all had one of course, because it wasn't possible to be there in the midst of all those food smells without eating something. Leigh had enough money so each of us got a paper cone piled a foot high with billowing pink cotton candy. Sis

169

telling Mattie her tongue looked as red as an apple got her giggling. Dissolving into sweet grit, the candy left a sticky red goo on my fingers that got stickier when I tried to lick them off with my sticky red tongue.

Tripp and Mattie soon lagged behind us. Because I was looking back at them while walking too close behind Leigh, I bumped into her when she stopped to yell, "Hurry up, y'all," at them.

Poor Tripp tried mightily to pull Mattie along, but she looked at everything except where she was going. When we stopped to wait for them, the midway crowds bunched up around us like the water in a stream surging around a boulder, which earned us some angry complaints.

When Tripp caught up with us, Leigh told him, "We've got a problem."

"You try getting her to go faster."

"It's not that," Leigh said. "I saw Mrs. Gonzalez up ahead and I think she saw us. If she thinks we're here alone she'll call Momma."

"I told you this was a dumb idea."

Grinning mischievously, Leigh's turned toward Sis. "You're not gonna like this, Sarah."

"What won't I like?"

"I'm going to tell her you're a friend of Momma's, and that you brought us to the fair."

Not only was Sis much too shy to play that game, but I'd never, ever, heard her lie to anyone about anything.

Sis was refusing to do it when a woman behind her said, "Leigh, I thought I recognized you and Tripp. And this must be Mattie. My but she sure has grown."

Leigh introduced Sis to Mrs. Gonzalez as a friend of her mom's. Mrs. Gonzalez asked Sis how she knew Aunt Helen. I had to turn around so Mrs. Gonzalez wouldn't see me stifling a laugh.

After a suspiciously-long pause, my red-faced sister said meekly, "From church."

Mrs. Gonzalez did a double take. Sis had goofed, that was

obvious. Leigh saved her butt by telling Mrs. Gonzalez we were late to meet some kids at the 4H barn.

As soon as we were out of sight of Mrs. Gonzalez, Leigh told Sis, "I think you cooked our goose."

"Why, what'd I do?"

"Mrs. Gonzalez goes to the same church we do."

Sis frowned at Leigh. "How could I possibly have known that?"

It wasn't surprising to see Sis so mad, considering Miss "I've never told a lie before" had been forced to tell a lie. Hell, even I know not to talk to Southerners about church or religion. That time I was smarter than Sis.

Leigh said, "We're wasting time" then walked away.

Tripp took Mattie's hand and followed her. Sis and I brought up the rear.

Leigh stopped near a shooting gallery to wait for us, telling Tripp when he and Mattie caught up with her, "I bet I'm a better shot then you are."

"Are not."

Mattie tugged on Leigh's shirtsleeve. "I want to shoot."

Leigh told her she was too short. "You can't even see over the counter. Besides we don't have time."

Mattie screamed, a long, loud, murderously high-pitched shriek, a crazy overreaction, even for Mattie. Little did I realize she'd seen something that had terrified her.

MATTIE SCREAMS

It was freaky the way Mattie grabbed Sis around the waist, whimpering and sniveling and making such a fuss that the people around us stopped to look. Sis picked Mattie up to quiet her down. With their arms wrapped tightly around each other, Mattie began sobbing, leaving tear tracks through the crusted dirt and cotton candy on her cheeks.

Telling Mattie, "There's nothing to be afraid of," Sis tried to pull Mattie's arms loose, but Mattie clung to Sis like a barnicle. Sis asked her what was wrong.

After pointing at the ground between our feet, Mattie yelled, "Snake" then buried her head in Sis' shoulder again.

Looking down I saw a snake as thick as my arm. I jumped back and screamed, well more of a shriek actually. Tripp knelt down and reached into the grass. I held my breath. I couldn't believe he dared to do that. I waited for the snake to strike him. When Tripp touched it I darn near feinted.

He grinned at us, said, "It's just an electric cable."

I bent down for a closer look. Sure enough, I'd made a fool of myself by screaming like a little kid. My face felt hot as road tar on a sunny day.

Although Mattie stopped crying, she clung on to Sis for dear life, and if I didn't know better, I'd have thought that Sis was enjoying Mattie's desperate affection. Of course, maybe I misread the distant look and faint smile on Sis' face. But I had to admit that being the one Mattie ran to when something frightened her would be kind of cool, like being a real-life hero.

With the scare over. I expected Sis to put Mattie down. She didn't. Mattie pulled back and looked at Sis, their faces an inch or two apart. They stayed like that for several moments. Then Mattie, acting as though she'd just woken from a dream, told Sis to put her down.

No sooner did her little feet touch the ground than Mattie pointed at a girl about Leigh's age carrying a stuffed teddy bear twice her size and said, "I want one."

"Forget it," Leigh told her, forcefully, which I didn't think left any room for argument.

But that didn't stop Mattie from yelling, "Not until you get me one," so loudly it got us another audience of strangers.

"No," Leigh said, "and that's final."

"I'll tell Momma you brought me to the fair."

Tripp tried to grab Mattie's hand, but she twisted away and tucked her hands under her arms.

Leigh grinned at Tripp. "I guess you'll have to get her one."

"How am I gonna do that?"

Leigh gave him three one dollar bills. "They have 'em at the shooting gallery. You think you're such a good shot, you win one for her."

"You know that game is rigged."

Even I knew that the carnies rigged the game by setting the rifle sights crooked. It meant you had to figure out how far off the sights were and how to compensate by aiming farther up or down, and farther left or right. To make it even harder, the targets for the big prizes were moving, which made hitting one of them impossible unless you were Annie Oakley. Of course the girl carrying the stuffed panda was really cute. No doubt some carnie worker had given it to her hoping she'd go behind one of the rides with him.

"That's enough for three plays," Leigh said. "If you use two of them to figure out how crooked the sights are, you'll still have one chance to win her a teddy bear."

"I couldn't win one of those teddy bears if I had a hundred dollars, and you know it."

173

"Well you'd better, cause we both know what she'll be like if you don't."

Tripp scrunched his face into a super-frown. "Oh man, that is so unfair."

Leigh told me to go with Tripp and Mattie.

"Why? I can't shoot."

"You can keep an eye on Mattie while Tripp's shooting"

That meant I'd be watching her when she had her big melt-down because she didn't get a teddy bear.

"Yeah" Tripp said, "And after I don't win the bear, then what?"

"Virgil's gonna be at the beer tent." She pointed down the path in the direction we'd been going. "It'll be down that way, off by itself. Look for us near there."

She didn't wait around for an argument. Sis hurried after her. Mattie grabbed Tripp's hand and practically dragged him back to the shooting gallery. I followed them.

Back at the shooting booth Tripp gave the carnie guy a dollar then pointed at a big stuffed panda bear hanging from the ceiling and asked him, "What do I have to do to win that?"

The carnie guy was grinning when he handed Tripp a rifle. "All you gotta do is knock down the four targets on the top row."

"How many tries do I get?"

"There's four shots in the gun."

Tripp muttered, "Ah jeez," as he placed his elbow on the stand to line up his first shot. It hit the wall an inch to the left of the nearest target.

"Oh poopy, Tripp," Mattie said. "You already missed one. Now I'll never get a teddy bear."

"Give me a chance to sight the gun in, Mattie."

Making a bigger-than-life pouty-face then saying, "You promised me," Mattie stepped back, getting caught and carried along by a crowd of rowdy, junior-high aged kids passing by, like catching a bug in your hair when you're riding your bike. I should have grabbed her and pulled her back but I'd been caught off-guard. I hurried after them.

I was able to follow by catching glimpses of Mattie's boots through the throngs of legs and shoes. I had just about caught up with them when it happened. Mattie saw Virgil. She ran right up to him, swung her leg back and gave him a swift kick to the chin then yelled, "You killed Dana and Uncle Pete."

"You're too smart for your own good," he said, scooping Mattie up, pinning her arms against him. Then he spotted me, and Grinning wickedly, said, "I bet this here brat will change her tune after she swallows some swamp water."

Then they disappeared into the torrent of people on the midway. Jostling my way through the crowds earned me all kinds of angry comments, but I lost track of them anyway.

I ran into Leigh and Sarah soon after that, which was a worry because I knew what Leigh's first question would be. "Where's Mattie?

"I lost her."

"What? How?"

I told her about the crowd of kids.

"Where's Tripp?"

"I don't know. I didn't wait for him. I went after Mattie." Poor Tripp, once again it wasn't his fault, but, once again, he'd be in serious trouble.

"And you couldn't stop Virgil?"

I shook my head. Her question had sounded more like an accusation. I already felt bad enough; wished I'd done a better job of watching Mattie, wished I'd been quicker to go after them. At least I knew where Virgil was going. "He said something about taking her to the lake."

Leigh said, "Damn," as the color drained from her cheeks.

"Mattie accused him of killing Dana and your uncle Pete."

"Oh God," Sarah said, frowning mightily. "We have to get help, Leigh."

Leigh shook her head. "No. We have to go the lake. No telling what he might do to Mattie before help gets there."

Sis was right to tell Leigh, "We don't stand a chance against Virgil."

"Yeah okay, fine. Go find a phone. Call my folks. I'll take Leonard with me."

Sis told me to be careful. I think she was actually worried about me, but not half as worried as I was.

I suggested to Leigh that we look for Tripp, because, "We'll need his help with Virgil."

After saying, "We don't have time for that," she headed toward the carnival entrance.

Back in the truck, both of us out of breath, Leigh's grip on the steering wheel was white-knuckle tight. She mashed the gas pedal down. The truck lurched forward. I asked her what she planned to do when we found them.

"I don't know."

Not the best answer. Unfortunately, the drive lasted long enough for me to imagine all sorts of horrible endings.

AMU'S CROCODILE

Even driving crazy-fast, at least ten minutes had passed before Leigh turned onto the Williston Cutoff. A minute later she turned into a pasture and began honking her horn. I asked her why.

"We're getting Amu."

He was standing on the dogtrot when we got there. Leigh told him we needed his help.

"What for?"

"The killer's got Mattie."

Amu climbed in next to me as Leigh got the truck rolling. He asked her where we were going.

"He took her to the lake. I'm afraid he'll drown her"

Back at the cutoff she floored it again, making the truck fishtail. I asked her how she knew where to go.

"I don't. We'll look for them where they found Uncle Pete's body."

At the same moment I spotted the car with the dumb-looking hood scoop parked off the road up ahead, Leigh locked up the brakes. Amu jumped out of the truck as it slid to a stop in the grass. Leigh and I followed. My hands felt sweaty. I got that weird "the ground is falling out from under me" feeling in my stomach.

Leigh stopped behind a line of bushes thirty feet from the lake shore. Through the bushes I saw Virgil holding a kicking, squirming Mattie at arm's length. Leigh told Amu and me to wait there until we got a chance to surprise him then stepped out of the bushes.

When Virgil saw her he said, "Well, lookie who's here."

Walking right toward Virgil, she told him, "Let her go."

"Don't reckon I'll do that," he said. "Killing your dog didn't do any good. So I reckon I'll up the ante."

She stopped an arm's length away from him, "You won't get away with it."

"Hell, they're gonna fry that half-wit for killing the sheriff. If they didn't get me for that, they won't get me for this neither."

I'd been counting on Leigh to do something heroic so I wouldn't have to. Now it looked as though I would, which couldn't possibly end well. My stomach churned like a cement mixer.

Virgil grinned at Leigh, said, "This mutt won't be so feisty after she drinks a little swamp water."

Then turning his back on Leigh, Virgil dragged Mattie, arms and legs flailing, into the swamp until her hair was floating in the foul-smelling black water, and backwash from his legs sloshed water into her mouth. As Mattie spit it out Amu ran out of the bushes yelling something that didn't sound like English.

As Virgil spun around and put his arm up defensively, he said, "Come any closer, I'll push her under."

Amu stopped, but not because of Virgil's threat. The sound of a splash, distant but loud, had stopped Amu in his tracks. We all looked, except Mattie who couldn't twist around far enough because of Virgil's grip.

A big, fast-moving mound of water was coming toward us, the wave spreading out behind it making a giant "V", like a motor boat's wake. But there was no boat, only a curl of water, as big as a pup tent.

Virgil dropped Mattie. She flailed and splashed and spit out swamp water. Maybe half a block away and moving faster than I could run, the wave had grown as tall as me and wide as a car, with white foam rolling in front of it.

Virgil started to back out of the water. When Mattie saw us looking at the lake she looked too, backing up when she saw the mound of water coming toward us. By then it wasn't more than a car's length away.

Everything that happened after that was over in an instant. The wave broke. An alligator as long as a bus crashed onto the shore not ten feet from Mattie. Poor Mattie was just a speck of a thing next to it. She should've run away. Leigh should have gone after her. I should have too. But we might as well have been cardboard cutouts for all the good we did poor Mattie.

Amu yelled, "Use your necklace, Mattie."

She held it out toward the gator.

Muttering something that sounded like gibberish, Amu scooped Mattie up in his arms, and clutching her in front of him, turned his back to the monster. Raised up on its legs is froze. Except for little waves lapping against the shore, there wasn't a sound, and for a while no one moved. Then Virgil ran for the bushes. Quick as a snake, the beast went after him, turning its head sideways, opening its jaws wide enough to swallow a steer. A mouthful of teeth snapped shut on Virgil.

On its way back to the swamp the beast opened its jaws and flipped its head back. Virgil slid deeper into its mouth. It clamped down again. Virgil went limp, but wasn't dead. With his face twisted into a silent scream, his eyes pleaded for help, a look I hoped to forget. Then, with Virgil hanging from its mouth, the beast turned around and slithered into the black expanse of the swamp.

With Mattie cradled in his arms, Amu told us we should go. "It might come back for me. Ours is an old score that's not settled."

Tripp might have been strong for his age, but Amu ran all the way back to my cousin's house carrying Mattie. On the way, Vigil's face kept appearing to me. I told myself that it could have been worse, that it could have been Mattie. Hell, it could have been me. The thought of being held in those teeth while I was alive gave me a serious case of the willies.

179

Amu put Mattie down next to the pasture fence behind my cousin's house. Leigh thanked him. He headed back to the cabin. Mattie walked the last few feet to their back door with Leigh and me, taking a hand from each of us.

REAL MAGIC

Tripp came out to meet us. He groaned, told Leigh, "We're gonna get whupped but good."

"Why, what'd you tell Momma?"

"Nothing."

"Then it'll be okay."

"No it won't."

"Why not?"

Tripp was telling Leigh, "Mrs. Gonzalez called," when Aunt Helen stepped outside, asked us, "Where the hell have y'all been?"

Leigh told her it was a long story.

"Well, you've got all the time in the world to tell it."

There'd be hell to pay. I could see Dad taking his belt off, could practically feel the sting of the leather.

Aunt Helen held the door for us. She cringed when Mattie walked past her. "What in the world did you get into, young lady?"

When Leigh passed her, Aunt Helen grabbed her arm. "You draw Mattie a bath and get her cleaned up. Then get yourself back here. I want to hear that story."

Sis and Tripp and I sat at the dining table to wait for Leigh and Mattie. Aunt Helen made herself some tea then joined us. The four of us waited in silence. It took a while for Leigh to get Mattie cleaned up enough to join us, and all that time I carefully avoided Aunt Helen's gaze for fear she'd ask me questions. I didn't want to tell her anything that Leigh might contradict later. Above all I hoped Leigh had thought of a clever explanation. If not, we were doomed.

When Mattie and Leigh joined us, Mattie was smiling. Leigh wasn't.

As Mattie climbed up on Aunt Helen's lap, Aunt Helen eyed Leigh with one eyebrow raised. "Well?"

"We went to the fair."

"I know. And I know Sarah told Mrs. Gonzalez some cockamamie story about taking you there."

Sis turned as red as a Santa Clause suit. Poor Sis. None of it had been her fault, and she wasn't even the one who told the lie.

And there was Leigh, like some fool kid reaching through the bars at the zoo to poke the bear, grinning at Sis in full view of her mother, until her mother said, "I know you think you're ever-so-clever, Leigh, so please explain to me how you took Mattie to the fair then brought her home smelling like the lake. And it had better be good, young lady, or there'll be repercussions."

Mattie asked her mom if they hurt.

"Does what hurt, dear?"

"Those things you said we'd get."

"You mean Repercussions?"

"Yeah, them."

"You don't need to worry about that. I know it wasn't your doing." Mattie settled back against Aunt Helen's shoulder. Aunt Helen focused her gaze on Leigh. "Well"

"It wasn't my fault."

"Oh? And whose fault was it?"

Leigh didn't answer.

Aunt Helen looked around the table. "I'm waiting."

"Ooh, ooh, I'll tell you," Mattie said, raising her hand, waving it so eagerly her butt wiggled Aunt Helen's lap.

As a warning to keep quiet, Leigh said Mattie's name as two syllables, the second one a whole octave higher than the first.

Smiling defiantly at Leigh, Mattie announced, "The man who took Uncle Pete's dragon held me in the swamp. That's how my hair got wet."

It got a gasp and a "Lord-a-mighty," from Aunt Helen.

So there it was. It was out and there'd be hell to pay. I felt faint.

Mattie told her mom, "But it's okay now."

"How can it be okay?"

"Because the alligator ate him."

Aunt Helen looked hot enough to cook eggs on her forehead after she heard that. "Would you care to explain that, Leigh?"

"It was Tripp's idea."

Aunt Helen sighed and shook her head then looked at Tripp. "Well?"

"Leigh was gonna quit. I couldn't let her do that."

"What are y'all talking about?"

Us kids sat there as still and silent as rabbits in a field hoping the fox won't notice them.

"This is your last chance, Leigh."

"We couldn't let Mr. Hammond get away with what he did."

"I don't care what he did. You wouldn't have put Mattie in danger if you'd left him alone like I told you."

"You're right. We should've quit when he killed Dana."

The way Aunt Helen gasped you'd have thought she'd just seen a dinosaur. "Virgil Hammond killed Dana?"

"Yes, ma'am."

"How do you know?"

"Leonard recognized his car when he hit Dana."

"It that true Leonard?"

"Oh yes, ma'am. He has a big ugly air scoop on the hood of his car. I bet there isn't another one like it in the whole world."

"Why in hell's burnt acre didn't you tell us?"

Leigh butted in to help me out "When I tried to tell you that you got mad. If you'd listened to me then, he wouldn't have kidnapped Mattie."

"Oh dear Lord. He kidnapped Mattie?"

"Yes, ma'am."

"At the fair?"

"Yes, ma'am."

"Weren't you watching her?"

Leigh could've thrown me to the wolves for letting Mattie get away. Instead she covered for me by telling her mom, "She got mad and took off and got caught up in a bunch of kids. She was gone in a blink."

Aunt Helen closed her eyes. I think she was counting to ten. "You kids shouldn't have gone to the fair, and you sure as hell shouldn't have taken Mattie with you. And why didn't you go get help?"

Leigh told her mom, "Sarah went to look for a phone so she could call you."

"I wasn't home. I went to the fair to look for you when Mrs. Gonzalez called."

"Well Virgil had already left for the lake, and I didn't think help would get there in time. Besides, we stopped on the way to get Amu to help us with Virgil."

"But be that as it may, it was a dangerous, foolish, thing you did."

Leigh started to say something. Her mom held a hand up to silence her. "Save it for when your father gets home."

Our mom would punish Sis and Me. And she'd rat on us to Dad. No telling what he'd do to us."

By the time we got up the next day Uncle Bud had eaten his breakfast and left to feed the cattle. I would've slept longer but Mattie came into our room and asked us if we were awake.

Tripp's half-awake answer was, "No. Now go away."

Mattie went out in the hallway and knocked on Tripp's door then came back in. "Are you awake now?"

"Jeez, Mattie, what do you want?"

"Mom told me to tell you guys that breakfast is ready."

I smelled pancakes and got right up.

Halfway through a pile of pancakes big enough to feed an army, Tripp asked Leigh, "So, is it true; what you told Dad last night?"

"Which part?"

"That a crocodile got Virgil."

Aunt Helen said, "You ask me, that whole story was mighty far-fetched."

Leigh told her that every word of it was true.

"Well, you're father heard from deputy Mayville this morning. He told us that Mr. Hammond is officially listed as missing."

Tripp asked Leigh, "So was it?"

"Was what, what?"

"Was it a crocodile that got him?"

"Definitely."

"How can you be so sure?"

"You mean, did it have a long skinny snout full of teeth that showed even with its mouth shut."

"Well, did it, Leigh?"

"It did."

"I wonder what it's doing so far north."

"I don't know, Tripp, I didn't get a chance to ask it."

"Well, I bet you're wrong."

"And I bet you're not as smart as you think."

Aunt Helen told them to go outdoors if they were going to argue about it.

My cousins rushed outside. After some serious discussion we decided that Mom and Aunt Helen were holding off on our punishment since that afternoon was our last one in Florida for the summer. You might think that was a relief, but we knew they didn't do it to be nice. It was just easier for them to let us play, especially since Mom had to pack for the trip back. We couldn't enjoy ourselves anyway, because we knew our punishments were going to hurt. I felt like Wile E. Coyote with an anvil hanging over me while I watched the rope unraveling.

Leigh said to Mattie, "You're awfully happy for someone

who's in trouble."

"Momma said it wasn't my fault so I won't get a spanking. Too bad for y'all, Mom said Daddy's gonna tan your hide." The little imp said that last part with a smile.

Meantime, we were faced with the same old problem - what to do. After checking for red ant mounds we lay down in the grass to think. I suggested we play tag. Mattie said she wasn't ever going to play tag again. Sis asked her why.

"It wouldn't be the same without Dana chasing us."

Tripp suggested we run through the sprinkler. I told him it wasn't hot enough for that.

Mattie held the necklace up over her head and fingered one of the tiny bones on it. "Aunt Sarah?"

"Yes, Mattie."

"Is this really magic?"

"If it saved you from that crocodile, then it must be."

"So it would it have eaten me if I didn't have this?"

That put Sis in a real pickle. If she answered "yes" Mattie would have nightmares about being eaten. But if Sis answered "no" she'd be admitting that she had just lied to Mattie about the magic.

Leigh came to her rescue. "Don't you worry, Mattie. If that old Croc had eaten you, he would've coughed you up like a hairball."

"Poopy-stink on you," Mattie said, standing up. "I'm never playing with you again, never, ever, ever. So there." Then she walked toward the pasture fence.

Leigh yelled, "Mattie, come on back. I was only kidding."

When she got to the fence, Mattie stood facing away from us with her head bowed down like she was praying.

"Jeez," Leigh said, sounding exasperated. "What's eating her?"

"Mattie admires you," Sis told her.

"You're crazy."

"It's true. That's why it's so easy for you to hurt her feelings."

Sis walked out to the fence and sat in the grass next to Mattie. I couldn't hear what she said to Mattie, but I saw her lips moving. I couldn't tell if Mattie answered because her back was to me, but she sat down next to Sis. Next thing I knew they were rattling on like old friends. I wondered who that was out there talking with Mattie.

AN UNEXPECTED LETTER

After lunch Aunt Helen sent Tripp out to get the mail. No one was more surprised than me when he announced that I'd gotten a letter. Other than Christmas and birthday cards, it was the first time I'd ever gotten anything in the mail, and it wasn't even my house.

After announcing that it was from Margo loud enough for everyone to hear, Tripp handed me the envelope. Margo's name was neatly printed in the upper left corner. I stared at it, dumbstruck.

Grinning like a fool, Leigh chanted, "Leonard and Margo sitting in a tree."

Aunt Helen told her to shush.

Mattie joined her for the, "K I S S I N G," part.

I went outside and sat on the front steps for some privacy. A moment later Sis appeared at the door. She sat on the steps next to me. "Well, what'd it say?"

"I didn't read it."

"Why not?"

"Margo probably sent it before Mom made that big scene at Grandpa's."

"The mail can't take more than two days to get here, so she must have mailed it after that."

188

I wanted desperately to read it, but was frightened of what it might say – that she might not want to see me ever again.

"Go on," Sis said, "Open it."

I opened it, and without thinking began reading it out loud. "It starts out, 'Thanks for the card.'"

I stopped reading then and looked at Sis because something didn't make sense. "Why'd she write that? I never sent her the card." As soon as I said it I realized what had happened. "You sent her the card, didn't you?"

She nodded her head.

"But what I wrote was crap."

"No it wasn't."

"Hey, you didn't tell Mom about me and Margo, did you?"

Sis shook her head.

"Then how'd you get Margo's address?"

"I asked Mom for Rena's address."

It was about the nicest thing Sarah had ever done for me. Just saying, "Thanks Sis," didn't seem like enough.

Sis asked if the card said anything else. I was still so flabbergasted that I read the rest of it out loud too. "She says she can't wait to see me next summer. She even asked me to write to her over the winter. But why'd she send me a nice card after what Mom did?"

"Because you were trying to do something nice for her when you got into trouble."

"Most kids would have laughed at me."

"She's smarter than that, Leonard."

"So being nice is smarter than being clever?"

"Maybe you do have good instincts after all."

"Huh?"

"Quit worrying about what other people think and be yourself."

"Be myself? But…"

She slumped forward slightly and her voice lowered a touch. "But what?"

"I can't be myself knowing she likes me. I'm afraid I'll do

189

something to make her not like me."

"Then I guess you have a problem."

"That's why I need your help."

She stood up. "Just be honest with her and you'll do fine."

She went inside then. I decided to write to Margo after I got back to New York. That would give me more time to think of something stupendous to write, and more chances to get help from Sis.

ONE LAST ADVENTURE

Aunt Helen sent us all outside and told us not to leave the yard. Mattie suggested we play leapfrog.

Leigh shook her head. "I still have a bruise from the last time you landed on me."

"Well, poopy."

Tripp, of all people, said "This is our last chance to do something before y'all go back to New York."

Leigh grinned at him. "You know we'll get one hell of a whupping if they catch us."

"A whupping's a whupping. It couldn't be much worse than the one we're already gonna get."

Leigh asked him what he had in mind.

"You're the one with the big ideas."

She grinned at him.

"You were already planning something, weren't you, Leigh?"

"Maybe."

"Well, what is it?"

"It's someplace special, probably the best thing we did all summer."

If she thought that would get me to go she was mistaken. Of course, if I didn't go, Aunt Helen would ask me why I came

191

back by myself and where the others were. So I agreed to go, because going was easier than making up a lie. Besides, I'm a terrible liar. Aunt Helen would see right through it if I lied to her.

Leigh asked Sis if she was coming.

"Not this time."

Mattie asked her to come with us, but not even, "Please, pretty please," changed Sis' mind. "Sorry Mattie, but we're in enough trouble already. I'll see you when you get back."

She left us to go inside. I'd known for a while that she was only a smidgen short of being a real grownup. She finally made it that summer, which was extra sad for me because she'd always been there to give me advice when things got bad. And I couldn't very well be buddies with a grownup; there are some things you just can't talk about with a grownup.

Mattie asked Leigh where "someplace special" was.

"You're gonna like it, cross my heart and hope to spit," which she did.

Mattie jumped up and down and clapped her hands. "Oh, Leigh, is it a fairy castle? Please say it is."

"If I told you it wouldn't be a surprise," Leigh said, smiling, and not just her usual grin, but a real smile. Then she crossed the bridge.

Mattie yelled, "Wait up, Leigh," cutting Tripp off at the bridge in her rush to catch up with her sister.

Instead of jumping the fence to wait for us on the other side, Leigh waited for us on the near side. Mattie took up her usual stance waiting for Tripp to hold the bottom wire up for her, but this time Leigh did it. At first Mattie looked at her sister with suspicion. Then she shrugged her shoulders and got down on all fours to scurry under the fence. Leigh backed up and took a running start, sailing over the fence, landing next to Mattie.

Then she and Mattie walked on ahead, hand in hand, Leigh at her usual quick pace and Mattie skipping along in her floppy boots, trying to keep up, hanging off of her big sister's words as eagerly as a dog begging for it's owners approval.

I ambled along by myself behind Tripp with my mind

wandering aimlessly through thoughts of the future, like: How bad would my punishment be? Would I get the belt from Dad? Would Amu still be there next summer and would Mattie still be his favorite? Was the crocodile that got Virgil real and would it be in the lake waiting for us next year? What would my life be like without Sis to talk to? Then, I thought about Margo and waiting a whole year to see her, and my heart ached.

Not even Leigh yelling, "Hurry up, Leonard," freed me from the thoughts I was having about Margo, some of them weirdly exciting, all of them confusing, one of them distressing - I still hadn't thought of something to write to her that would impress her. Having already told her in the card that I liked her and thought she was pretty, I wanted to think of something brilliant to write. I thought if I concentrated really, really hard, maybe... But deep down I knew that wasn't going to happen.

Knowing I wouldn't get a letter from Margo until I sent her something was what had me so upset. I couldn't wait a whole year for a letter from her. That was an eternity. I could fill a bunch of letters with the adventures I'd had with my cousins, but when I thought about telling her that stuff, I didn't get that weird good feeling, like sharing a special secret, that I'd gotten when I wrote in the card that I liked her.

Of course, I'd look pretty stupid if Margo didn't like me back. Maybe that was the point - taking a big chance, sharing my feelings without knowing it was safe. But how could I describe my feelings if I didn't understand them? At the rate I was going it would take me all year just to write one stupid word. I had to do better than that if I wanted to get letters from Margo this winter, and I wanted that more than I wanted anything, even more than one of those new three-speed English bicycles.

Discouraged and frustrated, I turned to the thought that made me happy no matter how bad I felt – Margo touching my hand. And of course that was the answer. I'd tell her how happy that made me. The thought of sharing that with her left me feeling as light and carefree as a cloud.

www.ingramcontent.com/pod-product-compliance
Lightning Source LLC
Chambersburg PA
CBHW071512170626
46811CB00007B/2828